"Everyone evacua...
There's a bomb," Izzy announced.

The police board members instantly ran from the room.

Izzy hurried to catch up to the K-9s and Austin. She stepped inside the bullpen.

Thor, the explosives K-9, sat a few feet away from a desk. Her desk.

It was then she noticed a backpack under her chair. A beeping filled the room, then intensified.

Izzy's heartbeat slammed in her chest. The bomb was about to blow.

The K-9s bolted toward the entrance, where Austin stood. The group scrambled to get away from the ticking time bomb.

They reached the exit, and Austin thrust open the door, hauling Izzy with him.

Seconds later, a thunderous explosion rocked the building, sending debris pelting through the station and out the shattered front glass doors.

The impact shoved Izzy to her knees on the snowy walkway. The attack revealed one thing.

None of them were safe...

Darlene L. Turner is an award-winning author who lives with her husband, Jeff, in Ontario, Canada. Her love of suspense began when she read her first Nancy Drew book. She's turned that passion into her writing and believes readers will be captured by her plots, inspired by her strong characters and moved by her inspirational message. Visit Darlene at www.darlenelturner.com, where there's suspense beyond borders.

Books by Darlene L. Turner

Love Inspired Suspense

Border Breach
Abducted in Alaska
Lethal Cover-Up
Safe House Exposed
Alaskan Avalanche Escape

Crisis Rescue Team

Fatal Forensic Investigation
Explosive Christmas Showdown
Mountain Abduction Rescue
Buried Grave Secrets
Yukon Wilderness Evidence
K-9 Ranch Protection

Visit the Author Profile page at LoveInspired.com.

K-9 Ranch Protection

DARLENE L. TURNER

LOVE INSPIRED SUSPENSE

INSPIRATIONAL ROMANCE

LOVE INSPIRED® SUSPENSE
INSPIRATIONAL ROMANCE

ISBN-13: 978-1-335-98014-4

K-9 Ranch Protection

Copyright © 2024 by Darlene L. Turner

Love Inspired
22 Adelaide St. West, 41st Floor
Toronto, Ontario M5H 4E3, Canada
www.LoveInspired.com

Printed in Lithuania

A man's heart deviseth his way:
but the Lord directeth his steps.
—*Proverbs* 16:9

For Helen, Melanie and Sara
You have blessed my life.

Acknowledgments

To my hubby: Jeff, thank you for putting up with my overactive writer imagination. I'm thankful that you get me. I love you.

To Valerie Beaman Miller: Thank you so much for letting me use Névé (and her name!) as the inspiration for my Alaskan malamute and for answering my questions. Anything I embellished for fiction is totally on me.

To my editor, Tina James, and my agent, Tamela Hancock Murray: You are both amazing and I'm thankful for your continual guidance.

To Sara Davison, Helen St. Martin and Melanie Stevenson: We've nicknamed ourselves the "Fab Four" as a joke, but I'm SO thankful God put us together. We fit perfectly.

Jesus: Thank You for always guiding my path. You've got me!

ONE

The computer screen flashed white and turned black. Constable Isabelle Tremblay's hand flew away from the keyboard and the hairs on her nape prickled. She glanced around the Harturn River Police Department's bullpen. All the monitors had gone dark. *Not good.* She shoved her office chair back and spun to her coworker. "What's happening?"

Before he could respond, menacing laughter exploded through their system, and a skull appeared on all screens. A message in bold red letters displayed beneath the frightening image.

IZZY, BACK OFF OR DIE.

A collective gasp filled the room.

Izzy bolted to her feet. She caught the meaning behind the message, and it confirmed her suspicions. Chief Constable Justin Tremblay's death wasn't from a heart attack.

Her father was murdered.

As quickly as the screens had flickered, they returned to normal. How had someone infiltrated HRPD's secure computer system? Their IT department was the best of the best. Plus she completed a double check recently of their firewalls. Her cyber knowledge verified they were impenetrable.

Or, at least, she thought so.

"Tremblay, my office. Now!" The voice of newly appointed Chief Constable Eric Halt boomed from the hallway.

"You're in trouble now," Constable Fisher said. "Did you click on something?"

She raised her hands. "No, I was just about to shut down for the day."

The older male constable clucked his tongue. "Well, I'm guessing from that message you're still secretly investigating your dad's death. You need to let sleeping dogs lie."

"I can't." Izzy shuffled through the hallway as her cell phone buzzed in her vest pocket. She ignored it and knocked on Chief Constable Halt's door.

"Enter."

Izzy inhaled and stepped into the office. "You wanted to see me?"

The chief lifted his index finger. "Thanks for the update. Make sure we're locked down. We can't let this happen again." He slammed the receiver back into the cradle and gestured toward the chair in front of his desk. "Sit."

Definitely not good. She obeyed.

Halt peeked over his reading glasses, eyes glaring. "Didn't I tell you to drop your investigation? This message tells me you didn't listen."

"Sir, I haven't used our department resources and have only investigated on my own time." She leaned forward. "Plus this message tells me I'm on the right track. Dad was murdered."

The man's eyes softened. "Listen, I'm really sorry about your father's death, but nothing suspicious materialized. He had a heart attack while driving and crashed. End of story."

Izzy was tired of hearing that lie. Even her own mother told her to back off, but Izzy couldn't. "He just had his annual physical and was in perfect health."

Halt drummed his fingers on his desktop. "Well, he was under a lot of stress the past couple of months. That may have triggered the attack."

Izzy shook her head. "It didn't. I figured out from his journal notes he was investigating some sort of drug cartel. Do you know anything about that?"

The chief constable stopped drumming his fingers. "No. What else did you find?"

"The rest of his notes are in code. That's what I'm trying to ascertain."

"Odd." He pointed to his phone. "Well, IT informed me that someone clicked on a link included in a fake company email sent to all of us. Whoever sent it is good. The bogus link unleashed a virus. Did you?"

What? "No. That email came in just as I was shutting down to leave for the day."

He crossed his arms. "Well, IT narrowed it down to your computer. Are you absolutely sure? Don't lie to me."

She popped to her feet. "I. Did. Not. You know I have—"

"I know. I know. Your partner told me about your memory. Must be nice to never forget anything." He tapped his thumb on the desk. "I'll get IT to investigate further. We need to determine where the virus came from and if it has compromised our system." He placed his hand on the phone. "Dismissed."

Izzy left the office, his words lingering in her mind.

Must be nice to never forget anything.

Some days Izzy wanted to forget. However, her hyperthymesia prevented her wish from becoming a reality. Having a perfect memory had certainly given her an edge when solving cases in her hometown of Harturn River, British Columbia, but it had also been the brunt of continuous jokes throughout her life. To where she tried to keep her condition a secret. Until her ex-partner, Austin Murray, convinced her to use her detailed memories to their advantage.

Her cell phone buzzed again, thrusting her out of thoughts of the past—and Austin—the man she *had* tried hard to forget. Unsuccessfully.

She fished out her device and swiped the screen.

Sims. Her father's confidential informant.

Figured out the cipher.

Izzy sucked in a breath. Sims came through. Now she'd be able to read her father's final encoded entries in his journal. Perhaps his notes would lead her to his killer.

Good. Off shift. Where can we meet?

Three dots bounced on her screen as she waited for his answer.

1 hour behind Chuckie's Bar and Grill. Bring the journal.

Izzy tapped in her last message.

See you soon.

She hurried back to her desk, gathered her belongings and snatched her winter coat from the back of the chair before leaving the police station.

A brisk wind slapped her in the face, chilling her instantly. She wiggled into her coat and zipped it all the way to her neck before putting on her gloves. She underestimated the expected change in weather. The temperature fell, meeting the meteorologist's forecast of a cold snap in February in British Columbia.

She jogged to her vehicle and pressed her key fob to unlock the door. A piece of paper stuck under her windshield wiper caught her attention. A wind gust flipped the top half over, revealing a message.

We're watching.

She bristled and peered around the lit parking lot. Nothing suspicious materialized. Izzy lifted the wiper and removed the note. Only the simple two-word message appeared on the paper.

However, the underlying threat seeped off the page. Whoever hacked into their police system wanted to ensure she understood their order to stay away.

But *they* underestimated the Tremblay determination flowing through her veins. The threat only escalated her resolve to find her father's killer. Izzy suppressed the trepidation threatening to overpower her thoughts, shoved the note in her purse and climbed into her SUV. *I'll find your murderer, Dad, if it's the last thing I do.*

Forty minutes later at her house, Izzy finished scanning the last pages of her father's journal. She would not risk losing any valuable information if something happened to the book. Especially now that she was close to deciphering its contents. Her father must have suspected the threat on his life as he'd mailed the journal to her condo's address the day before his death. Because of this, she was positive it contained valuable information that would uncover his killer and what he'd been working on. Izzy yanked the thumb drive from her laptop as her eyes shifted to the brown journal sitting on her desk. A thought tumbled into her mind.

Keep the two separate.

But where should she hide the drive?

She spotted her father's box of items from the police station, and an idea formed. Izzy took out his favorite coin from its pouch and dropped in the drive. She wouldn't hide it inside her condo because that's the first place anyone would search. Izzy put on her jacket and placed the journal in her purse. She stuffed the thumb drive in one coat pocket and her bear spray in the other. Being off duty meant she had to leave her weapon behind, but the repellant would at least give her some type of protection. Izzy snatched her key fob and raced outside to hide the drive in her favorite spot in her backyard. Somewhere no one would think to look.

She turned into the darkened alleyway and parked her SUV

beside a dumpster fifteen minutes later. Before exiting to meet Sims, she punched in her partner's personal cell phone number and waited.

"Hey, Izzy, what's up?" Constable Douglas Carver asked.

The man's experience had impressed her throughout the past few years, and she needed his advice. Plus his fatherly demeanor comforted her after her own father's death. "Doug, I have a lead on the cipher to decode Dad's notes. I'm about to meet with Sims but wanted to see if you could come too. I need your help."

"I'm in a meeting with Austin Murray going through pictures of his dogs. Halt tasked me with buying one for the K-9 unit. Where are you?" The concern in his voice filtered through the phone.

Izzy stiffened at the mention of her ex-partner's name. Austin Murray's failure to act at a crime scene had robbed their police station of Sergeant Clara Jenkins—Izzy's best friend and mentor. Clara died that night from a gunshot wound to the chest. Ten years had passed since Austin quit the force, and Izzy had stayed away from the man, even with Harturn River's small population of thirty-five thousand. Izzy had secretly fallen for her partner, but the pain of losing Clara caused Izzy to suppress her true feelings for the man.

She was aware of his K-9 ranch which also included horses, cattle, and other farm animals, but had purposely avoided going there. She bit her lip. "I'm behind Chuckie's Bar and Grill about to talk to Sims. How much longer will you be?"

"Izzy, what's going on? I can hear the concern in your voice."

She explained the events of the past hour, including the note on her windshield. "Sorry I didn't contact you earlier. There wasn't time. I could use your years of expertise. And backup, of course."

"Are you calling me old?" His teasing tone made her smile.

"Never."

"On my way. Don't do anything stupid." He clicked off.

A door slammed nearby, startling Izzy. She turned and spied Sims lighting a cigarette beside the bar's back entrance. She studied the surroundings before hustling to his side.

The informant puffed out a cloud of smoke. "'Bout time you got here. You bring the journal?"

She patted her purse. "Yup. Where's the cipher?"

He tapped his temple. "In here."

Izzy gritted her teeth. How had her father put up with this man? His cocky attitude had annoyed her over the last week. She found Sims's number hidden under the inside tab of the journal's cover. Her father had spoken of the man often and how he'd helped him put away many criminals, so she called Sims. Right away, he agreed with her suspicions of foul play in her father's death. "Sims, please tell me what you discovered."

He took one more drag of his cigarette before dropping the butt to the ground and stepping on any remaining embers. "It's really quite simple. Your dad always loved his books. He used the book cipher. Show me the journal."

Izzy withdrew the book and opened to a page containing her father's cryptic notes of numbers. "There's a number at the top that doesn't seem to follow the same sequence as the others."

"Interesting." Sims pointed. "I believe these numbers mean the page, line and word needed to decipher the message. You just have to figure out which book and edition he used."

Izzy palm-slapped her forehead. "Of course. Why hadn't I thought of that? How did you figure it out?"

"I remembered something he said to me the day before he died. He said he loved the way Sherlock used a book cipher in one of his novels."

"Right. *The Valley of Fear.* It was Dad's favorite." She latched on to Sims's arm. "Wait, do you think he used that book for the cipher?"

He shook his head. "Doubtful. Too easy. Since he sent the journal to you, it's a book only you would guess."

"Right." Izzy's memory pictured every book on her shelves, but nothing stood out.

"Don't limit it to your current bookshelf. Go way back, it could—"

A shot pierced the frosty night.

Sims dropped.

"No!" Izzy fell to her knees and placed two fingers on his neck. No pulse. She hung her head. The man was gone.

Movement rustled behind her.

She jumped upright and pulled out her bear spray, still clutching the journal.

"Don't even think about it," a sinister voice said. "I have a Glock pointed at you. Drop the can and turn around slowly."

Bear spray couldn't outrun a bullet. Izzy obeyed and turned to face her attacker.

The man stood away from the bar's back entrance light, concealing his identity. However, something about his voice triggered a memory. A meeting at HRPD's station behind closed doors six months ago. She had caught a portion of the conversation as she left the building. The angry words surfaced in her memory. Even though the speaker had lowered his tone, she didn't miss the whispered words.

He can't find out.

The sentence returned, but she couldn't assign the voice to a name. Had the person lowered their pitch tonight to disguise themselves?

"Toss the journal on the ground and kick it to me."

A phrase her father used to say came to mind.

Izzy always give an assailant what they ask for. Your life isn't worth it.

Besides, she had scanned the contents. She did as the attacker commanded.

"Now the drive."

She chewed on the inside of her mouth, contemplating how

they acquired that information. "What drive?" She had to stall for time. *Doug, where are you?*

"Don't play coy. You're your father's daughter. Of course you made a copy."

"Did you kill my father?" She held her breath in anticipation of the man's answer.

"Give us the drive. Now!"

"Who's us?" she asked.

Rough hands grabbed her from behind and spun her around. "Me." He punched her in the face. "Tell us, or you'll get a worse beating."

She stumbled backward, her hand flying to her nose to ward off the sting. Blood oozed between her fingers. "I—I—don't know—"

Her father's words returned, but she ignored them. She couldn't lose the drive too.

The man raised his cell phone, showing her a picture of the texts Izzy and Sims had exchanged earlier. "We know you did as we've been watching." He raised his opposite fist to give her another blow.

This time, she blocked the punch.

His phone fell to the snowy pavement, but he stood his ground.

She stared into his face. A face her perfect memory would remember if she lived through the attack.

Pounding footsteps echoed in the alley.

She pivoted.

A blunt object came down hard on her head from behind. She spun and caught a reflection in the window of someone witnessing the exchange. Someone she didn't expect to see. *No!* Spots exploded and her knees buckled.

Her attackers fled into the shadows.

"Izzy!"

Her name registered, and she turned toward the voice as her vision faded.

A face passed under the light.

Austin?

Pain splintered in her head moments before her world went dark.

Austin Murray fell to his knees in front of his ex-partner, checking for a pulse. *Please, God. Help her be okay.* Steady. *Thank You.* "Doug, her vitals are strong."

Doug squatted in front of the man and drew in an audible breath. "This is Sims, her father's CI." He placed his fingers on the man's neck. "He's gone. Gunshot wound to the forehead." Doug withdrew his cell phone and stood. "I'll call it in." He stepped toward the bar's back door, requesting emergency services.

Austin examined Izzy's face. Blood dripped from her swollen nose, but a punch probably wouldn't have knocked her out. He gently turned her head and ran his fingers along her neck in search of a second wound. His fingers stopped at a bump forming at the back of her head. Austin fisted his hands, heat flushing his cheeks. Someone had beaten her up, but why?

You didn't make it here in time. He had failed her.

Again.

His mistake ten years ago had not only caused her to pull away, but was the reason he left the force to work on his father's ranch. He couldn't face the harm he'd inflicted. He'd frozen during a call that cost the life of Sergeant Clara Jenkins—Izzy's best friend.

An object to the right caught his attention, bringing him out of the past. He pushed himself upright and leaned down for a better look.

A cell phone lay face up with the cracked screen illuminated, revealing a conversation between Izzy and what Austin guessed was the CI named Sims.

Doug returned. "Paramedics and officers are on the way."

Austin pointed. "This must be Izzy's phone."

The older constable shook his head. "Nope. Hers has a bright pink cover on it."

Pink. Her favorite color.

"Sims, perhaps?" Austin asked.

Doug adjusted his winter gloves and moved to the CI's body. He patted the man's pocket, then took out a phone. "Nope. His is here."

"Odd. Maybe one of the attackers?" Austin reached for the cell phone, but snapped his hand back. *Don't contaminate the scene.* "Do you have an evidence bag on you?"

Doug extracted one from his winter jacket. "Of course. A cop's habit." He squatted in front of the phone, leaning closer. "Wait, these texts are between Izzy and Sims. How did the attacker get them?"

"Didn't you say someone hacked into HRPD's system earlier? Perhaps they got into Izzy's phone too."

Sirens blared nearby.

"Yes, and she also mentioned someone left her a note on her SUV's windshield stating they were watching." Doug read the screen before snapping a picture. He dropped the phone into a bag and placed it back on the ground. "Don't want it to get wet with the snow. The crime scene unit will want to see everything where it was. They'll then take it to our digital forensics team." He circled the area where Izzy had fallen, studying around her body.

"What are you looking for?" Austin asked.

"Did you see her father's journal? That's what Sims is referring to in the text. He was helping her with a cipher."

"I didn't see it when I arrived." Austin's gaze flicked back at Izzy, emotions bubbling inside. They had been partners for two years and had bonded to the point where he had strong feelings for her. Feelings he'd never acted upon since they worked together. Seeing her unconscious with a bloody nose heightened his desire to protect her. "Who could have done this? Who's watching her? Maybe her attackers took it. I realize I'm not a cop any longer, but can you give me a hint of what she was investigating?"

Doug placed his hands on his hips. "Can't you guess? Against Chief Constable Halt's advice, she's been looking into her father's death on her own time."

Austin had attended Chief Constable Justin Tremblay's funeral, but kept his distance as much as possible. He only offered Izzy and her family brief condolences before leaving the church. "But didn't he die in a crash caused by a heart attack?"

Doug nodded. "His wife, Rebecca, was in the car. She said he cried out before clutching his chest. The car veered toward the ditch and she failed to stop the crash. Fortunately, she only had minor injuries."

"So why was Izzy investigating his death?" Austin trusted Izzy's instincts and perfect memory, so she must have had a reason to doubt the findings.

Doug knelt beside his partner and shook her. "Come on, Izzy, wake up." He turned back to Austin. "She claims her father just received a perfect bill of health after his annual physical. She spieled off everything her father had told her about his doctor's visit. You know her memory."

Austin didn't miss the concern in the older man's eyes. "You're close to her, aren't you?"

Sirens intensified, and the flashing lights lit up the dark alley.

"Yes." Doug brushed a lock of Izzy's brown hair from her forehead. "I took her under my wing after—"

"After I screwed up."

The ambulance pulled into the alleyway, followed by a police cruiser and forensics van.

Doug stood. "I wouldn't put it like that. We all make mistakes, son."

"Well, mine cost Izzy's friend her life." Austin would never forget the look on Izzy's face from that night. Her pained expression revealed a mixture of anger and surprise, speaking volumes.

She had blamed him.

Doug grazed Austin's arm. "She eventually forgave you."

Austin highly doubted it. How could she when he still struggled with the guilt?

Voices jarred him from the past.

Two paramedics and multiple officers filled the area.

The bar's back door opened and screeching loud music filtered into the alleyway. A man emerged. "What's going on here?"

Doug approached. "Sir, stay back. Police need to cordon off the crime scene."

The burly man's eyes widened in the bar's back light. "Crime scene?"

"Didn't you hear the shot?" Austin asked.

He gestured through the open door. "With all the loud music? I saw the flashing lights from the front entrance."

One paramedic squatted in front of Izzy. The other checked Sims's pulse and shook his head.

"Get back inside, but don't leave the premises." Doug turned to an approaching officer. "Constable Fisher, can you escort this man back into the bar and question him?"

The constable eyed Izzy. "Is she gonna be okay?"

"Paramedics are checking her now," Doug said. "Go inside."

Austin relocated to Izzy's side. "She took a blow to the back of her head. I felt a goose egg."

The paramedic nodded. "Good to know. Doctors will check her for a concussion." He turned to his partner. "Vitals are strong. Let's get her to Harturn General."

"Can I come with you?" Austin suddenly felt the need to be by her side. Whoever had attacked her could still be watching.

"Are you related?"

Austin suppressed a sigh. "No, but—"

"I can vouch for him." Doug removed his cell phone. "I'll get her mother to meet you at the hospital. I have to finish up here. Let Austin go with her. I want someone she knows by her side in case she wakes up in the ambulance. I'll get Halt to send a constable to protect Izzy. Someone has obviously targeted her."

Thirty minutes later Austin paced outside the emergency room's doors. Since he wasn't family, they wouldn't let him inside, but her mother and sister arrived fifteen minutes ago. He had asked one of them to update him, but Rebecca Tremblay's curt greeting didn't give him much hope of that happening.

But he couldn't leave without knowing Izzy was okay.

Austin plunked himself into a chair, leaning forward on his knees. *Lord, please help Izzy be okay and protect her from whoever is after her. I want to help. No, I need to help. I believe You've brought her back into my life for a reason. Show me what that is.*

Austin's cell phone buzzed. He dug it out from his pocket and checked the screen. His ranch foreman. Austin was supposed to call him an hour ago. "Sawyer, I'm so sorry I didn't call. I'm at the hospital."

"What? Are you okay?" he asked.

"It's not me. It's Izzy. She's been hurt, and I was with her partner when she called him." Austin recounted to his ranch foreman and best friend, Sawyer King, what happened. "I'm waiting to get an update on her condition. I'm worried, bud. Someone is targeting her. She needs protection."

"The police will help her. You're not part of the force any longer, bro."

A young boy and a woman shuffled into the packed emergency waiting room. The boy held a washcloth over his nose.

Austin stood and pointed to his chair. "You can sit here."

The woman nodded and smiled. "Thanks."

The emergency room doors opened and Izzy's sister, Blaire, gestured for Austin to come.

"Sawyer, I gotta run. I'll be back as soon as I can. Can you feed the dogs?" Austin hated when he had to miss their feeding frenzy. It always made him smile.

"Of course. I'll pray for Izzy." He clicked off.

Austin shoved the phone back into his pocket and followed Blaire. "What's going on? Is your mother aware you're bringing me in?"

Izzy's younger sister turned. "Doesn't matter what she thinks. Izzy is awake and is asking for you."

Austin's jaw dropped. "She is?"

"Yes. She said she saw your face in a dream."

What? "A dream?"

"The constable outside the door said you were at the crime scene, so perhaps she saw you before she passed out?" Blaire stopped and turned. "Mom is quite upset, of course, with Dad just passing. Please be sensitive. She's in a foul mood."

"I understand."

She continued down the hallway.

A hooded man talking on a cell phone with his head down whisked by Austin, knocking into his shoulder. He glanced up. "Watch where you're going, man."

Austin raised his hands. "Perhaps you should listen to your own advice."

"Whatever." He cussed and continued down the hall. "Quit worrying. I took care of him. She's here and I'll get it out of her. I promise."

Austin didn't care for the man's menacing tone. Coincidence?

"You coming?" Blaire asked.

He shook off the thought and followed. *You're too jumpy.*

They walked into Izzy's room.

Blaire gestured toward him. "I found Austin."

Izzy's eyes widened. "Hey, you."

Austin hurried to her side and took her hand in his. "You

okay? I was so worried when I found you unconscious in the alley."

"The alley?"

"You don't remember?" Odd. She never forgot anything.

"I. Don't. Know." Izzy rubbed her temples. "Something's wrong with me. This has never happened before."

"What was the last thing you remember?" he asked.

She looked around the room. "A virus got into our system before my shift ended."

Austin checked his watch. He knew their shift times. "Izzy, that was three hours ago. You're telling me you don't remember going to meet Sims at the back of Chuckie's Bar and Grill?"

She bit her lip as tears trickled down her cheeks. "No."

Rebecca Tremblay caught hold of Austin's arm. "Please tell us what's going on. The constable wouldn't divulge anything, and now I can't find him."

"Wait, Doug said they would send someone to protect her." Austin rushed back through the doorway, glancing left, then right.

The corridor was empty.

I took care of him.

Was the man referring to the constable?

Izzy was still in danger.

And it was up to Austin to protect her.

TWO

Izzy didn't miss Austin's right brow rise in bewilderment. She remembered that trait from when they were partners. He had left the room abruptly, then returned with a haunted expression. "What is it, Austin?"

He looked at Izzy's mother, then back. "You're in danger."

Her head pounded not only from the goose egg, but from the confusion rolling around her brain. "What makes you say that? You're scaring me."

"You really don't remember?"

Frustration tightened her chest. Missing a period of her memory had never happened to her before, and she didn't like it. It was as if a piece of her had vanished. "I don't. Tell me."

Austin moved closer to her bed. "You called Doug while I was meeting with him about my K-9 dogs. You asked him to meet you behind Chuckie's Bar and Grill and said your CI found the cipher to your father's notes. Doug was concerned, and I went with him to help. When we arrived, we found Sims with a GSW to the forehead and you were unconscious."

Panic elevated her heartbeat, increasing the beeping coming from the monitor beside her. "I don't remember any of that."

Izzy's mother rubbed her arm. "Austin, you need to leave. You're raising her blood pressure."

"Mom, this proves to me that Dad didn't die by accident. Someone targeted him." Izzy focused on Austin. "What else do you know? Where's Doug? Is he okay?"

"He's fine and still at the scene. We found a phone beside you that displayed the texts between you and Sims. Somehow, your attacker hacked into your phone and got the information. They ambushed you and shot Sims." He pointed to her purse sitting on the rolling table. "Listen, is your father's journal in your bag?"

She reached her hand out. "Pass it to me."

"Sister, you need to rest," Blaire said. "This is too much. The doctor said you have a concussion."

"I need to know, Blaire."

Austin passed her the purse.

She opened it and rummaged through it. "It's not here. Neither is my phone."

Austin shifted his stance. "Doug removed your phone from the outside pocket since we're pretty sure someone hacked it. He was taking it to digital forensics."

"Makes sense." Izzy took out a piece of paper. "What's this?" She unfolded it and bold letters screamed at her.

We're watching.

"That's the note you told Doug was under your windshield wiper when you left the station." Austin turned to Izzy's mother. "Mrs. Tremblay, we need to get her somewhere safe."

Her mother placed her hands on her hips. "What makes you so sure she's not safe here?"

"Because I heard an odd conversation from a man in the hallway stating 'he'd get it out of her.'"

"That may mean nothing," Blaire said.

"Yes, it could, but he also said 'he took care of him.'" Austin air-quoted the words *took care of him*. "And now, I can't find the constable I'd seen come into the hospital. He rushed through the emergency doors after flashing his badge."

"I spoke to him earlier." Rebecca Tremblay tapped her manicured nails on her chin. "I thought he just went to the bathroom."

Izzy sat up and swung her legs over the edge of the bed, waiting for the sudden wave of dizziness to subside. "I have to get out of here."

Her mother darted to her side. "Izzy, you need to be in the hospital."

Izzy struggled to contain her emotions. "Mom, you don't get it. Whoever killed Dad is now after me. I need to leave."

Blaire snatched Izzy's bag of clothes from the chair. "Are you coming home with us?"

"I can't. That will only put you in more danger. I can't go to my condo either." She directed her attention to Austin. "Ideas?"

"You're asking him? Do you remember what happened ten years ago? We don't even know if the conversation he heard was about you." Her mother's angered questions blared in the small room.

"Mom. Stop. I trust his instincts." She stood but swayed.

Austin wrapped his arm around her waist. "Come to my ranch. These people don't know me. You'll be safe there."

His nearness brought back the feelings she had suppressed over the past ten years. Feelings she had never admitted to him— or even herself. She had cared deeply for Austin, but refused to act on her emotions because of their working relationship. She hadn't wanted to put anyone in jeopardy.

And now…her ex-boyfriend Dax's obsessiveness had deterred her from getting into any relationship with a man. Her heart couldn't take it.

However, Austin's solution would put him back into her life. Could she handle being so close to him again? Sure, she had forgiven him for Clara's death, but still didn't know why he froze that day. He had kept that piece of information to himself. Why?

She swallowed the thickening in her throat, yanking herself from the past. She had to concentrate on the here and now.

And finding her father's killer. For all of their sakes.

"Yes, that makes sense." Izzy took her bag of clothes from her sister. "Mom. Blaire. You can't tell anyone where I'm going. Got it?"

They nodded.

Izzy read the angst in their contorted expressions. "It will be okay. We'll get through this." She brought them both into a group embrace. "I'll keep in constant touch, but I need to figure out what happened in the past three hours. Something tells me my locked memories hold the answers to Dad's killer. I just have to unlock them."

After picking up a new cell phone and clothes at a local store, Izzy massaged her temples as Austin drove through the log gate of Murray K-9 Ranch. Izzy had called Doug, requesting he meet them at Austin's home. She wanted to find out more of what happened at the crime scene. Austin had shared everything he saw, but Izzy's three-hour black hole remained closed.

The doctor hadn't liked her demand to leave the hospital, but once she explained the danger to herself and his staff, he relented. Her head scan revealed only a mild concussion, and her symptoms had lessened, so he gave her instructions to stay awake for a few hours and have those around her monitor her before sleeping. Austin had reassured the doctor he had a former military medic on his grounds, and he'd have him ensure she was okay.

Izzy observed the log ranch house in the distance as they drove down the long driveway. Even in late evening, the well-lit home revealed its beauty. She had visited the ranch many times before that devastating event ten years ago. She could rhyme off every detail in each building.

So, why couldn't she remember the missing three hours? The doctor had explained it may have been the blow to the head, or the trauma of the event, or a combination of both. Izzy guessed the latter.

Snow blanketed the grounds, generating a peaceful atmosphere. Ranch hands walked horses into the stable to the left of the main house. Another stable containing cattle and other animals was nestled on the north side of the property. A building to the right wasn't in her memory bank. "What's over there?"

"My K-9 kennels and training facility." Austin hit a button and the middle garage door opened. "That's right. I added to the buildings after I left the force."

"How many dogs do you have here?"

He parked and switched off the engine. "Right now, we have eleven, including my favorite dog, Névé. Her name means snow in Latin." Barking came from within the ranch house. "Speaking of her. She lives in the house and has a special place in my heart. I bonded with her after finding the pup abandoned on my property four years ago. We've been inseparable ever since. The rest are in the kennels. Are you okay with dogs?"

"Of course."

"Awesome. You'll fit in nicely then. Let's get you settled inside. Doug should be here any moment." Austin exited his F150 truck.

Izzy followed just as the door leading into the ranch house opened and a slender, muscular male stepped inside the garage.

A dog bounded around the man, then ran toward Austin, barking.

"Hey, baby girl." Austin squatted and the K-9 snuggled close, licking his face. "I missed you too." He pushed himself to his feet. "Izzy, meet Névé, pronounced 'nay vay.'"

Izzy held out her hand.

Névé sniffed before plowing into Izzy's legs. Izzy stumbled backward and giggled. "Whoa, girl."

"Névé, sit," Austin commanded.

The dog obeyed.

"Good girl." Austin reached into his pocket and tossed her a treat. "Sorry, she gets overzealous sometimes. She's not a great watch dog because she loves people, but she's strong and can rescue."

"She's beautiful. What type of dog is she?"

"Alaskan malamute." Austin gestured toward the man. "This is my ranch foreman and best friend, Sawyer King. Sawyer, meet Constable Isabelle Tremblay. Sawyer lives in the loft on the top level. He's an ex-medic, so he can make sure you're okay."

He approached and held out his hand. "Nice to meet you, Isabelle."

She returned the gesture. "Please call me Izzy. Sorry for intruding."

"Don't be silly. Happy to have you. Austin explained what's going on. I've alerted the ranch hands, and we're here to protect you too." Sawyer turned to Austin as a buzzer sounded. "That's probably Constable Carver. I'll let him in and then head to the loft. See you in the morning. Nice meeting you, Izzy."

"You too."

"Thanks, bud," Austin said. "I appreciate all your help."

Sawyer saluted and retreated into the house.

Austin walked to the back of his truck and lifted out Izzy's shopping bags. "Okay, let's head in and I'll show you to your room."

Izzy followed Austin and Névé into the large ranch home, stopping in the entrance. "Wow. You've made extensive changes since I was here last." She studied the log beams and ceiling.

"A fire gutted the upper level five years ago, so I renovated." He gestured to the log stairs. "I'll put you upstairs. Follow me."

Izzy trudged up the steps with Névé at her heels. Seemed the dog wanted to be in their presence.

Austin stopped in front of a middle room and opened the door. "Here we are. Get settled." He set the bags on the log-framed bed.

Izzy entered the room.

A cowbell clanged, the sound resonating into the second level. Izzy startled.

Austin caught her arm, pulling her into a strong hold. "Sorry, I forgot to warn you of my doorbell. You okay?"

His woodsy scent weakened her resolve to alienate herself from him. She broke their embrace. "It just startled me. My nerves are a bit on edge."

"You're safe here, Izzy."

Was she?

Maybe safe from her father's killers, but what about her heart?

Austin juggled three mugs of tea in his hands and set them on the dining room table. "Here you go. They're decaf."

Izzy and Doug huddled together, perusing the crime scene pictures the constable had brought with him. Izzy shifted her glance upward and smiled. "Thanks." She took the green mug and sipped.

Austin ignored the sudden hitch in his heartbeat. *Concentrate. She's here for protection, not you.* "How are you feeling?"

"The dizziness has subsided, but not the headache. I just took more pain meds." She addressed Doug. "Let's get started. I'm sure the pills will kick in soon, and I won't be able to concentrate any more than what my fuzzy brain can now."

Austin sat and checked on his dog.

Névé lay in the corner on her mat, snoozing. Content with no cares in the world.

The life of a dog. Austin sipped his chamomile tea. "You guys okay if I sit in on your discussion? I realize I'm not an officer any longer, but I can still offer my help."

"Well, since Dad's case isn't an official investigation, I don't see why not." Izzy placed her finger on a picture of the cracked cell phone. "I don't remember this text conversation with Sims." She huffed and sat back in her chair.

Doug squeezed her shoulder. "Don't try so hard. It will come back to you." He picked up another picture. "Do you remember bringing bear spray with you to the alley?"

She shook her head. "I don't even remember going to the alley. Like I said, the last memory I have is of the virus shutting down our system." She fingered her tiny loop earring. "Wait, I remember evil laughter before a message appeared on every monitor."

"What did it say?" Austin asked.

"'Izzy, back off or die.'" She turned to Doug. "That's a start, right? I didn't remember that before. Perhaps by tomorrow, my memories will return."

Would that mean you don't need me any longer?

Wait, where had that thought come from? The Izzy that Austin remembered didn't need anyone for anything. Her independent nature and smarts stood out to him when they worked cases together. But they were also what made him secretly fall for her.

Don't go there. He needed to shift his thoughts. "Doug, did you find the constable that was supposed to be guarding Izzy at the hospital?"

"Yes. We found him unconscious in a utility closet. He didn't see who knocked him out."

"Not good." Austin pointed to the cell phone picture. "Have they been able to get prints off the phone?"

"Still working on it." Doug faced Izzy. "Here's what we pieced together. Sims told you he found a cipher and asked you to bring your dad's journal to the alley behind Chuckie's Bar and Grill. You called me when you arrived and told me about the meeting, requesting my help. That's when Austin and I left for the bar." He took another sip of tea as if gathering his next thoughts carefully. "Sims was shot, and you were attacked before the suspects took off with the journal."

"And that's when we arrived," Austin added. "We didn't see anyone else at the scene."

"Constables canvassed the area but found no leads. Fisher spoke with the bar owner. The man missed the entire exchange. Claims his loud music drowned out the shot that killed Sims." Doug tapped his thumb on a picture of the bar's back entrance. "I wonder why Sims chose this location. Do you have any idea, Izzy?"

She placed her hands on the table and pushed herself upright, then paced around the room.

Austin remembered the habit well. It was her way of picturing details from her memory.

She stopped beside Névé and squatted, petting the dog.

Woof! Névé lifted her head and licked Izzy's face.

Austin's heart warmed at the exchange. He could get used to the two girls bonding. *Stop.* He stared into his cup of tea while he waited for her response.

"I remember Sims told me he used to meet regularly with Dad there. Why, I'm not sure." Izzy returned to the table. "Does Halt know yet how HRPD's system was hacked?"

"No. IT and digital forensics are working together on it." Doug gathered all the pictures and stuffed them into a file folder. "It's getting late and you need your rest, Cinderella."

"Funny. Stop calling me that. You know I hate it." She finished her tea and pushed it aside. "And yes, I remember that detail."

Doug stood. "Okay, I'll reconnect with you tomorrow."

Izzy's azure blue eyes brightened. "Maybe if I go home and look through my condo, it will bring back some memories. I must have returned there before going to see Sims, as I wasn't dressed in my uniform."

Doug shook his head. "That's not wise. If they hacked your phone, they probably also have your address."

Izzy crossed her arms. "But I have to know, Doug. Something there might unlock those three hours."

He reached out and grasped both of her arms. "I need you to be safe. Stay here." He shifted his eyes to Austin. "Please make sure she listens."

Did the man *know* his partner? When Izzy made her mind up on something, no one could stop her.

Especially when it came to her father. They'd had a close relationship. If Justin Tremblay had been murdered, Izzy would rearrange the universe to find the culprits.

Of that, Austin was certain.

And he'd help her.

Austin chuckled. "I'll do my best, but you know her stubborn nature."

"Yeah, that's what I'm afraid of." Doug tapped the folder on the table. "I'll leave this here, as the pictures may spark your memory." His cell phone buzzed, and he unclipped it from his belt, swiping the screen. "Good news. Got a hit off the print on the phone. Ex-con named Ned Bolton. Izzy, that ring a bell?"

She gasped. "Yes. That's Sims's former prison mate. That can't be a coincidence."

"Nope. Fisher is getting a warrant for his arrest."

"I want in on the interrogation." Izzy raised her hands. "And don't say no. We can figure out a way to get me to the station incognito."

Doug pursed his lips. "I realize I can't convince you otherwise, but get some rest tonight." His phone buzzed again, and he swiped the screen. "No!"

Névé hopped to her feet and barked.

Austin tensed.

Izzy latched on to Doug's arm. "What is it?"

"They got to me, too." He raised his phone to show them the screen.

Tell Izzy, we WILL find her.

Austin's pulse thrashed in his ears.

No one was safe. Would the suspect discover his ranch, too?

THREE

Austin nursed a cup of strong coffee the next morning as he waited for Izzy to get up. The text from the suspect took them all by surprise and she couldn't wind down, but paced the living room. She finally went to bed after midnight. He prayed she at least got a few hours of rest. He barely slept. Having her back in his life after ten years kept him awake, thinking about her safety. Thankfully, Sawyer helped Austin ensure the ranch was locked up tight.

Névé hovered at Austin's feet, staying by her master. She had obviously sensed the tension radiating from both him and Izzy.

Austin reached and stroked her ears. "You're a good girl."

Woof! She snuggled closer before lying down.

Austin opened the police folder Doug had left and examined the pictures one by one, hoping to gain some insight into what had happened to Izzy. After five minutes, the only thing Austin gained was fury toward whoever had attacked his ex-partner. He slammed the folder shut and squared his shoulders, determination setting in to help Izzy find the suspects and protect her.

"What did that folder do to you, bud?" Sawyer entered the dining room, holding a steaming cup of coffee.

Austin leaned back in his chair and folded his arms. "Sorry. I'm just angry over whoever did this to Izzy."

"No need to apologize. I understand. I remember you telling me what she meant to you." Sawyer's eyes remained on Austin. "Your expression reveals that she still does."

Austin drank from his mug to subdue the feelings obviously showing on his face. He had to keep them in check. Izzy probably still blamed him for Clara's death, even though Doug had said differently. How could she not? Austin did.

He blew out a breath. "Seeing her unconscious last night hit me hard, bro."

"I get it, but please be careful. I remember what you went through back then."

Sawyer had just started working for Austin's father when the incident that ended Austin's policing career happened. The two became best friends quickly and Sawyer was now Austin's right-hand man in both friendship and Austin's K-9 training business. He also oversaw the ranch. "I will. I just need her to be safe."

"Well, she is here. The ranch hands have all agreed to keep their eyes open and protect her." Sawyer stood. "Speaking of them, I must get our daily chores going. You feed the dogs?"

"Done. Depending on how the day goes, I may give them a break from training." Austin finished his coffee and rose, heading toward the kitchen, but stopped at the window. "Looks like twenty centimeters fell overnight. Did the contractor plow the laneway?"

"Yes, they came in the early hours. I'm about to help the guys with the entrances. Just needed some fuel." Sawyer chuckled and took another drink.

"Good, thanks."

Névé barked and hopped up, darting toward the entrance.

Izzy appeared in the doorway, rubbing her eyes. "Morning." She squatted and kissed Névé's forehead. "Hey, girl. Happy to see you, too."

Did Izzy realize how cute she looked in her sleepy state?

Austin's eyes shifted to Sawyer.

His friend gave a slight head shake. His meaning coming loud and clear.

Keep your distance.

Austin cleared his throat. "Izzy, how are you feeling?"

She gave the dog another kiss and rose to her feet. "A little better. I fell asleep finally."

"Good. How about some coffee and breakfast?"

"I'm heading to the stable to help the guys shovel." Sawyer stood. "Morning, Izzy."

"Morning. Sorry, I didn't mean to interrupt."

"You didn't." Sawyer slapped Austin's back. "Remember what I said. Text me if there's anything you need, bro."

"Got it." Austin turned to Izzy. "Bacon and eggs?"

"Sounds delightful, but you don't need to go to all that trouble for me." She wrapped her sweater tighter around her waist.

"No trouble. I have a fire going in the living room if you want to warm up while I make breakfast."

Her cell phone buzzed. She removed it from her sweater pocket and swiped the screen, reading. "It's Doug. They found Ned and are bringing him in." She tapped in a message before dropping the phone into her pocket and cementing her stance. "Austin, I need to be there. Ned may have information about my father's death."

So much for a hearty breakfast. "Do you think that's wise? You'll put yourself back in their sights if the suspects are watching the station, which they most likely are."

"I know, but I need to question him."

"Can't they conference you in?" How could he make her understand the danger she was about to put herself in? "Would your chief constable even allow it? You're too close to it and wouldn't be able to remain objective."

Her eyes flashed. "Don't tell me I can't remain objective after what happened with Clara."

Névé whimpered.

Austin winced and raised his hands. "Sorry. You're right. None of my business. I just don't want to see you get hurt."

Her shoulders slumped forward, tears pooling. "Sorry, Austin. I didn't mean that. I just need to find out what happened to my father. And to me in those three hours. Maybe Ned knows something."

Austin could never resist this woman. Plus he guessed she'd probably sneak out on him, and go anyway. Best help her do it safely.

He eyed his dog, and a plan emerged. "Okay, I have an idea. Doug wanted me to bring some of my K-9s into the station. How about I take Névé here and some others? I can give you some rancher clothes and a hat to disguise you as one of my workers. You up for some spy work?"

Her eyes brightened, and she lunged forward, throwing herself into his arms. "Thank you!"

He stumbled backward at her sudden movement, but caught his footing, holding her tight. His stomach fluttered at her closeness. *Step away.* He jerked back, staring into her face. "But we'll need Doug's approval first."

"Of course. I'll call and convince him right now."

"You will. No doubt in my mind." He chuckled. "Okay, there's some yogurt and fruit in the fridge. You eat and I'll be back with your disguise."

Fifty minutes later, after loading three dogs in the back of his K-9 vehicle and driving to the HRPD police station, Austin parked in the building's rear lot.

The door opened and Doug appeared, gesturing them inside.

Austin shut off the engine and turned to Izzy. "Since Névé has bonded quickly with you, I'll let you take her by the leash. Keep your head down. If these people hacked into your system, they may have eyes inside. We need to keep your identity hidden. Got it?"

She yanked her tuque down farther on her head, then tucked her hair inside before putting on wide-rimmed reading glasses. "Got it."

Sawyer had helped gather her disguise of a bulky plaid flannel shirt, jeans, work boots, and a man's winter jacket and hat. Hopefully, it would help with their ruse.

"Let me get the dogs out. I'll bring them to your side." He didn't wait for an answer, but hopped out and around to the back. He opened the cages and secured the leashes for Névé, Goose and Thor. "Come."

The dogs jumped down and trotted behind him as Austin moved to the passenger side.

Izzy climbed from the vehicle.

Austin handed her Névé's leash. "Let's go."

The duo rushed forward with the dogs and entered through the door Doug held open.

"Thanks, Constable Carver, for agreeing to meet my dogs." Austin raised his voice in case anyone was watching or listening. He gestured toward Izzy. "This is Bud. My ranch hand."

"Your dogs are beautiful." Doug held out his hand to Izzy. "Good to meet you, Bud. Come with me."

They advanced farther into the station, and Doug leaned closer to Izzy. "Halt isn't happy about this, but approved it. Let me do the talking, though. It was the only way he'd let you in the room."

"Understood."

"No one else knows you're coming. I've put Ned in the farthest interrogation room." Doug turned to Austin. "Take the dogs into the observation room next to it. Can you keep them quiet?"

Austin didn't like leaving Izzy, but had no choice. At least he'd be able to hear and see everything going on. "Absolutely, unless they alert to danger. That's how they're trained."

A man dressed in a suit opened a door at the other end of the corridor, gesturing a woman inside. Chatter escaped into the hall from those already gathered. She turned her head and Austin recognized Harturn River's mayor before she entered HRPD's boardroom.

Doug pointed. "There's an early morning board meeting at

the other end, so we have to tread carefully. They're always watching."

Austin, Doug, Izzy and the dogs proceeded through the area, passing a couple of constables.

The pair nodded a greeting to Austin and Doug, but didn't even look twice at Izzy.

Clearly, her disguise was working.

But would she be able to stay quiet and fool the man who had attacked her?

Izzy tugged at her hat, ensuring any hairs at the back of her neck were hidden before she slouched and shuffled into the interrogation room behind Doug. She had to conceal everything about her identity, including her body language, if they were going to trick Ned Bolton.

The man was slumped forward, his wrists handcuffed to the metal bar attached to the table. He rested his head on his hands as he snored.

How could he sleep at a time like this? Irritation exploded in her chest, and she struggled to keep her anger from lashing out at the suspect.

Doug slammed his police folder on the table, jarring the convict from his snooze. "Sorry for waking you, Ned." Doug's sarcastic tone blared in the small room. He wiggled the handcuffs. They clanged on the metal bar. "We need your undivided attention."

"Huh?" Ned yawned and sat upright. "Why am I under arrest?"

Doug gestured for Izzy to sit as he dropped into one of the two chairs across the table from Ned. "This is Detective Bud. He's interested in your case."

Izzy took the chair to the right, turned it around and straddled it. Maybe a bit dramatic, but she had to think like a man. She nodded.

"You going somewhere?" Ned gestured toward her winter coat.

"He's getting ready for an early takedown." Doug took out an evidence bag from his pocket and shoved it in front of Ned. "Recognize this?"

The man's eyes bulged. "You found my phone. Thought I lost it in a bar."

Gotcha. Obviously this thug wasn't firing on all cylinders and definitely not the leader of the supposed drug cartel Izzy's father had been investigating. A leader would know better than to identify property held in police custody. Perhaps this would be easier than they thought.

Izzy analyzed Ned Bolton's face, hoping to jar any memories of what happened last night. The only evidence that remained for her was the bruise on the left side of her nose and a lump at the back of her head. Thankfully, she concealed the black and blue with makeup.

The scrawny man tapped his thumb on the table, jiggling the cuffs. He leaned forward, and a long wiry red curl sprang out from under his baseball cap. His wrinkled plaid flannel shirt gaped open because of a missing top button, revealing a soiled white T-shirt underneath.

Clearly, not a criminal mastermind, but what connection did he have to the crime scene?

"So you claim this is your phone?" Doug asked.

"Yup."

"You admit you were at a crime scene where we found this?"

Once again, his eyes widened. "Wait, what? No. I lost it."

Likely story.

Doug flicked his eyes to Izzy, then scowled.

He wasn't buying it either.

Doug continued to address Ned. "Do you know Constable Isabelle Tremblay?"

The man looked left and shifted his gaze to the floor. "No. Should I?"

Izzy cleared her throat, signaling her partner to probe further.

Doug bolted out of his seat.

His sudden action startled even Izzy. Seemed her frayed nerves were still on edge from the man's attack.

Doug walked to the mirror where Austin watched from behind, then turned. "You're lying. Were you hired to beat her up?"

"I ain't sayin' nothin'."

Doug approached the table. "Let me see your hands."

Ned cowered, attempting to hide them.

Doug pointed at the man's reddened knuckles. "You get that from punching her in the face? You're going down for assault—and murder."

He straightened. "What? She's dead? She wasn't when I—"

Izzy chuckled. *Gotcha. Again.*

The man gave her the once-over. "Why ain't you talkin'?"

Oops.

"He's only observing today." Doug smirked and placed his hands on the table, leaning into Ned's personal space. "So you were there? Come on. We don't want you. We want your leader."

Good diversion, partner. Izzy had almost blown it by not concealing her girlish chuckle.

Ned bit his lip.

Doug inched closer. "Who killed the man we found shot to death? Was it you?"

Ned's jaw dropped and he recoiled, distancing himself from Doug's forceful question. "No! It was him."

"Him who?"

Ned blew out a ragged breath. "Don't know his real name, but…" He looked around the room and then leaned forward. "He could be watching. He has spies everywhere."

Doug's eyes snapped to Izzy's.

Not good.

Doug placed a notebook and pen in front of Ned before uncuffing him. "Write what you know."

Ned took the pen in his left hand and scribbled on the page.

The action propelled a scene into Izzy's head.

A left hand flying toward her face in the dark.

A memory from last night?

Izzy massaged the left side of her nose. More than likely, Ned Bolton had been her attacker.

"Tell me who this is?" Doug turned the notebook in Izzy's direction, and she caught the name on the page.

Padilla.

"The one who hired me to beat up the cop," Ned whispered.

"Beat her up, but not kill her?" Doug asked.

"So, she's not dead. Good. You can't charge me with murder then." He rubbed his throat. "I'm thirsty. Give me a drink and I'll tell you everything."

"Tell us what you know first. Then I'll get you a drink and something to eat." Doug tapped the name Padilla written on the page. "Okay, tell us exactly what this person hired you to do."

"Be his muscle and help get information out of her."

"His muscle?"

How could this small man beat anyone up? Izzy fingered her nose. Then again, he had a good left hook.

"Don't let my size fool ya." Ned flexed his biceps. "I might be small, but I'm mighty. Friends called me Scrapper for a reason." He coughed before wiping perspiration from his forehead.

Were they making him nervous?

Doug tucked the notebook back in his vest pocket. "Alrighty then. Tell us what information he was looking for."

"He took her journal but wanted a thumb drive." He raised his hands. "That's everything. Are you going to release me—"

One of Austin's dogs barked from the other room.

It was alerting, but to what?

Ned's jaw dropped. "You have a dog in here?"

Doug stood. "Bud, let's check out what's going on." He turned to Ned. "We'll be back."

They entered the corridor, and Izzy opened the observation room door, sticking her head inside. "Is one of your dogs alerting to something?"

Austin stiffened. "I trained Goose in tracking. Névé in search and rescue. Thor in…" His eyes widened.

Izzy grabbed his arm. "What?"

"Explosives." He turned to Doug. "You need to evacuate the building and notify the bomb unit."

Doug nodded. "I'll gather our prisoner and get everyone out." He spoke into his radio as he ran back into the interrogation room.

Austin nudged Izzy. "You need to get out. Thor can find the bomb." He engaged his dogs. "Come!" He unleashed the German shepherd. "Thor, seek!"

The K-9 barreled down the hallway and stopped in front of the boardroom, barking. He raised his snout, circled and took off running again.

Were the police board members still in there? Izzy had to warn them. She thrust open the door. "Everyone, evacuate the building. Possible bomb."

Mayor Fox sprang to her feet at the same time as Izzy's Uncle Ford.

Vincent Jackson—her father's best friend—rose. "How did someone get a bomb in here?" His tone demanded an answer.

Izzy didn't have time to explain. "Not sure, sir. Please evacuate."

The rest of the members screamed and scampered from the room.

Austin released the other two dogs. "They're not trained in explosives, but can certainly help. Seek!"

Goose dashed in the same direction.

Névé stayed by Izzy's side.

Izzy observed the malamute. "She's not a protection dog, right?"

"No, but she senses danger from the other two and likes you. I need to follow the dogs. Evacuate." Austin ran toward the station's front office where Goose and Thor had headed.

"Not a chance." Izzy followed with Névé at her heels.

Constables and HRPD's civilian staff hustled to the exit. Their tortured expressions revealed everyone's horror. Izzy couldn't remember a time when their station had been attacked in this magnitude.

Was it all her fault?

Thor's heightened bark cut off her thoughts.

Izzy hurried to catch up to the K-9s and Austin. She stepped inside the bullpen.

Thor sat a few feet away from a desk. *Her* desk.

"Thor, Goose, retreat!" Austin's forceful commands stopped Izzy in her tracks.

It was then she noticed a backpack under her chair. A beeping filled the room, then intensified.

Izzy's heartbeat slammed in her chest. The bomb was about to blow.

The K-9s bolted toward the entrance where Austin stood. He turned. "Get out!"

Beside her, Névé growled and latched on to her coat, tugging her back into the hallway. The group scrambled to get away from the ticking time bomb.

They reached the exit and Austin thrust open the door, hauling her with him.

Seconds later a thunderous explosion rocked the building, sending debris pelting through the station and out the shattered front glass doors.

The impact shoved Izzy to her knees on the snowy walkway. The attack revealed one thing.

None of them were safe from Padilla.

FOUR

"Good job, guys. You saved lives today." Austin ruffled Névé's fur with one hand and Thor's with the other as he waited for the paramedics to examine Izzy. If Thor hadn't alerted to the bomb, things may not have turned out well at HRPD's station. Goose snuggled closer and Austin chuckled. "You too, boy." *Thank You, Lord, for my dogs.*

Everyone had evacuated in time, and the explosion had been isolated to the front of the building. Austin and Izzy had a few minor cuts, and the dogs appeared to be fine. However, Austin had arranged for his vet to meet him back at the Murray K-9 Ranch. Austin would not take any chances with his dogs.

Firefighters had arrived and extinguished the flames. The bomb unit had also determined there were no more explosives on the property. Austin concurred as he had commanded Thor to seek, but the German shepherd hadn't alerted to any further dangers.

A crowd now gathered in the parking lot. The board members had remained at the scene along with constables and civilian workers. Even the cold February temperature didn't deter the multitudes from checking out the explosion.

Izzy shook the paramedic's hand and then approached Austin. "I'm good to go."

Austin noted the bandage over her right brow. "You sure about that, especially after what happened yesterday?"

Névé left Austin's side and nestled next to Izzy—her new favorite spot.

And that warmed Austin's heart.

Izzy bent down and petted the malamute's head. "Hey, girl. Thanks for saving my life."

Thor barked.

Izzy chuckled. "You too, Thor." She turned to Austin. "I'm impressed by your training. These dogs are so smart."

"Thank you. Speaking of them, we need to get back to the ranch, as I want the vet to examine them."

Izzy took off her hat and scratched her head. "Did they get hurt?"

"I think they're fine, but I don't take any risks with my K-9 family. So, let's—"

"Izzy!" A slender man jogged across the parking lot.

A balding man and a woman followed.

"Uncle Ford, I'm glad you're okay." Izzy wrapped her arms around the man.

He gestured toward the others. "You remember your dad's friend Vincent and our town's mayor, Georgia Fox?"

"Of course." Izzy shook their hands before gesturing to Austin. "This is Austin Murray and his K-9s, Névé, Thor and Goose."

Izzy's uncle pointed to her clothing. "What's up with the odd getup?"

"Just doing some role playing for an undercover mission." Izzy stuffed the hat into her coat pocket.

Good save, Izzy. She was still quick on her feet. Not only did she have a perfect memory, but her street smarts once again impressed Austin.

Georgia kneeled in front of the K-9s. "You saved the day." She looked up at Austin. "Good work."

Austin dipped his head. "Thanks, ma'am."

"I thought I'd heard a dog bark earlier." Vincent held out his hand. "Good you were here at the station. Odd coincidence."

Austin didn't miss Izzy's flattened lips and slight shake of her head. Even though they'd been apart for ten years, he still could read her like a proverbial book. Her expression held an obvious message.

Stay silent.

"Austin!" Doug practically skidded across to the group. "Thanks again for showing me your dogs. I'll give the chief constable an update, and we'll get back to you. These three sure proved their worth today."

Izzy's partner had perfect timing and was also keeping up with the ruse. Austin stuck out his hand. "Pleasure doing business with you, Constable Carver."

Doug shook his hand, then pulled back and snapped his fingers. "Wait. I need to talk to you about one more thing. Can you meet me around back at your K-9 vehicle? I want to discuss a visit to your training facility, but first, I have to consult with Constable Tremblay about her undercover ops."

Austin didn't miss the slight tilt of Izzy's head.

These two were good at playing the game.

It was clear they didn't trust anyone.

Doug turned to the board members. "Will you excuse us?"

"Of course." Ford grazed his niece's arm. "Stay safe, Izzy."

She nodded. "Glad to see you're all okay."

The mayor once again bent down beside the dogs. "We owe our lives to these fine animals."

All three barked as if agreeing to her statement.

The group laughed before trudging off toward the ambulance.

Doug inched closer to Austin and Izzy. "Sorry for the charade, but I didn't want them thinking you came here together."

"Good cover," Izzy whispered. "What do you have to report?"

"Let's head to Austin's vehicle." Doug looked around. "You never know who's listening or watching. Today's attack proves to me your father was on to something, Izzy. We need to take all precautions."

Izzy hissed in a breath and put the tuque back on.

Austin bristled, shivers snaking down his spine. He observed the onlookers. Was the culprit among them?

Urgency propelled him forward. He had to get Izzy back to his ranch. He tugged on his K-9s' leashes. "Come."

The group relocated to the side of the building, sidestepping any remaining debris. Thankfully, the blast hadn't reached the area where Austin had parked.

He clicked his key fob and released the hatch. "Up," he commanded his dogs. The trio hopped into their cages and Austin closed the doors. "Okay, what information do you have?"

Doug once again glanced around before responding. "Forensics reported the explosion took out the hallway and our bullpen. Seemed whoever did this only wanted to destroy part of the building."

Izzy latched on to Doug's arm. "How did someone get into the station so easily to set explosives?"

"Not sure. The only individuals I saw were our staff, constables and the board members. Do you remember seeing anything odd when you came in earlier?"

Izzy tapped her gloved finger on her chin. "I saw the mayor and Vincent go into the boardroom. Constables Fisher and Reynolds passed us in the corridor, but it's highly unlikely they'd do it."

"Well, we'll be questioning everyone in attendance at the station today." Doug stuffed his notebook into his pocket. "We'll also check video footage of anyone coming and going. If it wasn't destroyed."

Austin read the angst on her face. "We need to get you back to the ranch. And out of harm's way."

"Agreed. One more thing. Did Ned's interrogation spark any memory of that three-hour window?"

Her eyes brightened. "Yes, Doug. Thanks for the reminder. I remembered a left fist coming out of nowhere in the dark and punching me in the face. I noticed Ned wrote with his left hand. It had to have been him who attacked me."

"I'm going to consult with Halt to get him to check your father's reports on recent investigations. That might help figure out this case, and also lead us to this Padilla."

Austin shifted his stance. "Izzy, you don't know what case your dad was working on?"

"No. He wouldn't tell me. Normally, he would have assigned it to someone at the station, but he said this one was for 'his eyes only.' Not sure why." She bit her lip. "His notes revealed something about a drug cartel, though."

Doug's radio crackled. "Carver, Halt here. We've had reports of a suspicious hooded figure seen nearby. Officers are in pursuit. If Izzy is still here, get her to safety. Now!"

Their leader's voice sent chills throughout Austin's body. Chills not from the cold weather but the continued danger following his ex-partner.

"Iz, we have to go." Austin hurried to the passenger side and opened the door. "Get in." He raced to the driver's side.

She climbed into the vehicle. "Doug, send me regular updates. I want to monitor the case from Austin's ranch."

"You know Halt won't allow that." He sighed. "But I know you and your clever computer skills will get information. I'll see what I can do. I need to get Bolton in lockup. Stay safe." Doug closed the door and tapped on the hood.

Austin started the engine and sped from the station's parking lot with one thought stuck in his mind.

He had to protect the woman in the passenger seat with his life.

After cleaning up and changing from her annoying disguise, Izzy sat sipping a coffee in Austin's rustic living room. Névé had taken up residence at Izzy's side. Literally lying on top of her feet as if pinning Izzy down, preventing her from going anywhere. Did the malamute sense Izzy's desire to escape and dive headfirst into her father's case? Izzy hated that her hands were tied. She was good at what she did, and her sharp memory could help the team, but she also knew Chief Constable Halt wouldn't let her investigate.

But what was stopping her from doing her own sleuthing? On her own time? She popped forward, disturbing Névé's hold on her. *That's it. I'll request a vacay.* It wasn't like she didn't have banked time she could use.

Woof!

"Sorry, girl. I know what you're thinking. Stay out of it." Izzy rubbed the dog's fur. "But, I can't."

Névé tilted her head to the side, as if questioning her motives.

"Don't judge me, okay? I need to solve this case. Protect my family. If they came after Dad, what's stopping them from getting to my mom, Uncle Ford and Blaire?"

Woof!

Izzy pushed herself upright and walked to the window overlooking the extensive property. "I know. I know. I'll be careful." She examined Austin's ranch grounds. Snow had covered every inch and glistened in the sun's rays. *Beautiful. I could live here.*

Where had that thought come from? Being around Austin again had warmed her heart. The kindness and gentleness she remembered from when they were partners resurfaced, bringing with it the feelings she had once. *He didn't feel the same as you, remember?* He had cut off all ties after he left the force. If he felt the same way as she had, wouldn't he have tried to stay in touch?

Then again, your anger at Clara's death pushed him away.

Izzy had struggled with how that horrifying call played out. Izzy, Austin, and Clara had responded and Austin entered the apartment first. An abusive man held his bruised and battered wife at gunpoint. The events turned ugly when he pointed the gun at them, and Austin had froze for some odd reason. His hesitation allowed the man to get a shot off. A shot that killed Izzy's best friend and mentor.

Izzy had blamed him. At first. But after long talks with her father, she realized Clara's death wasn't Austin's fault. It was the angry man's fault.

But it had cost Clara her life. Izzy had forgiven Austin years ago, but that night still haunted her. Every detail. The abused wife's injuries. The man's red, angered expression. Clara's blood.

Izzy shut her eyes to block out the scene.

Why had she forgotten memories she wanted desperately to remember but she couldn't forget that horrible night?

Having a perfect memory had not only brought praise from her childhood schoolmates and friends, but ridicule. Because of that, Izzy had tried to hide her abilities, but soon realized she had a gift.

We don't hide our gifts. God gave them to us for a reason. Use it, Izzy.

Her father's words had encouraged her to take advantage of her sharp memory, so she did. But she also tried hard not to brag, as she'd seen jealousy over the years from friends, colleagues and even her sister, Blaire.

A ranch hand riding a horse appeared down the driveway, jolting Izzy from the past. *Concentrate.*

She fished out her cell phone, chose her leader from her list of contacts and waited for him to pick up.

"Tremblay, what's wrong? You okay?" Halt's tone conveyed his worry.

"I'm fine." She bit her lip and pushed away her trepidation at the question she was about to ask.

"You lying low?"

Her leader gave her the perfect segue. "Yes. That's why I'm calling, sir. I have vacation banked from last year and would like to take it now. Sorry for the short notice. Is that okay?"

Tapping filtered through the phone.

He was drumming his fingers on his desk. A habit she'd coined as his thinking pose.

She waited, knowing better than to interrupt him.

He puffed out a breath. "Fine. But Tremblay. Don't go investigating your father's death. It's too dangerous."

Seemed her boss was good at reading her thoughts.

"But if you do, be sure to give me updates."

Was he silently giving her permission?

She smiled. "Thank you, sir."

"Your dad would want me to protect you, Izzy. Please stay put." He paused. "And don't trust anyone, and I mean anyone." He clicked off.

Izzy froze. A shudder zigzagged up her spine. Chief Constable Halt had never called her Izzy, only Tremblay. *That* she remembered.

Did he know something she didn't?

"Did I hear you talking to someone?"

She pivoted, her hand flying to her chest. "Austin, you scared me."

He held out a plate of cookies. "Sorry. I brought you some homemade chocolate chip cookies. Your fave."

He remembered.

She snatched one and stuffed it into her mouth. "Mmm… so…good," she mumbled.

"Now, who were you talking to?" He set the plate on the log coffee table before sitting in a rocking chair.

"Well, first, Névé then Halt." She plunked down on the plaid couch.

Névé hopped up beside her.

Izzy ruffled her ears. "Are you allowed up here?"

Woof!

"She likes you, and yes, she's allowed." He snagged a cookie. "What did Halt say?"

"I asked him if I could take some time off. He said yes, but then warned me to stay away from the case."

"So, he knows you well, then."

"Yes, already. But then he gave me his permission without giving me his permission."

Austin tilted his head. "Come again."

She told him about her conversation with Halt, including his warning and the use of her given name. "Do you think he knows something about the case Dad was working on?"

"Possibly." He leaned forward, elbows to knees. "Iz, I know you and I'm positive you'll investigate the case. I'm not sure you should. You're too close to it."

She blasted to her feet. "How can you say that? I need to find out the truth, Austin. My father was murdered, and this person may come after my family next." She hated the tear that had just escaped without warning. She normally wasn't an emotional person.

He stood and brought her into a hug. "I'm sorry. I'm just scared for you."

Izzy melted in Austin's arms, and she wanted to stay sheltered there.

Don't trust anyone.

Halt's words returned, but surely he hadn't meant Austin. Did he?

Her cell phone dinged, and she retreated from his embrace. She removed the device, swiping the screen.

Izzy, don't think you or your family are safe. Don't investigate or Blaire is next.

Izzy's legs buckled, and she crumpled to the floor.

Névé barked, circling her as if in protection mode.

No! Lord, don't let them take my family.

FIVE

Austin squatted beside her. "What is it, Iz?" He petted the malamute before commanding the dog to sit. She sensed Izzy's distress and wanted to help.

Izzy raised her phone.

Austin read the menacing message. He balled his hands into fists, curbing his anger from bubbling to the surface. *Lord, protect the Tremblay family from this evil man.*

"Padilla is threatening Blaire. I have to get to Mom's. They need me." She tried to push herself up, but fell back onto the floor.

Once again, Austin brought her into his arms. "You do that and you might provoke whoever this is even more."

Her heart hammered in rhythm with his. "Iz. Breathe. In. Out."

She repeated the breathing technique multiple times before pulling away and standing. "I have to call Blaire."

"Understood. How can I help?"

She chewed on her bottom lip. "Can you call Doug? Get him to ask Halt to send patrols near Mom's place?"

"I will."

Névé brushed around Izzy's legs.

"I didn't think she was a protection dog." Izzy bent down and kissed Névé's head.

"She's not, but she senses your anxiety. Plus she likes you." He took out his cell phone. "I'll call Doug and also get Sawyer to ensure the property is secure."

"Thanks." She headed toward the kitchen but turned at the living room entrance. "Oh, I would like to set up a makeshift office where I can go over everything I remember of the case. I'm hoping maybe it will jog my memory. Where can I do that?"

Austin suppressed the urge to argue, but he knew it wouldn't do any good. "You can use my office. There's lots of room and two desks. Can I help? I know I'm not an officer any longer, but maybe a second set of eyes would help."

"Absolutely. I'd like that."

"There are lots of supplies in my office you can use to make up an evidence board if you want."

"Awesome, thanks." Izzy continued into the kitchen.

Austin turned to Névé and pointed at Izzy. "Heel." He didn't want Izzy to be alone. Even if the malamute wasn't a protection dog, she could provide company for Izzy.

He grabbed his two-way and hit the button. "Sawyer, come in."

Seconds later the radio squawked. "What's up?"

"Can you do another perimeter check? Izzy just got a threatening text." Austin walked to the window and peered out into his front yard. All seemed quiet, but he wasn't taking any chances when it came to Izzy's safety.

"Will do. She okay?"

Austin raked his fingers through his dark brown hair. "Shaken up. I'm worried about her."

"Understand. I'll report back in fifteen minutes. Taking Bucky out for a ride."

Sawyer had named the rescue horse a month ago, when Austin had brought the black beauty to the ranch. They'd been inseparable since.

"Appreciate it. I'll fill you in later."

"Copy."

Austin punched in Doug's number and waited.

He answered after the first ring. "Everything okay, Austin?"

"Not entirely sure." He explained the situation to Izzy's partner. "Can you send someone to Rebecca's home to double-check on her and Blaire? Izzy wanted to go, but I told her no."

"Let's hope she doesn't sneak out."

"I have my best spy at her heels. Literally." Austin pictured

Névé not letting Izzy out of her sight. It impressed him that the two had bonded so quickly.

"Good. She needs to stay put. I have Halt breathing down my neck." He paused. "Listen, she's probably getting ready to dive deeper into the case."

Doug knew his partner well.

"Yup. She's already asked for office space." Austin chuckled. "Don't worry. I'm watching, and I have informed my ranch hands of the situation."

"Good. Thanks for the update. I'll contact you when I have more information about her family."

"Appreciate it. Talk later." Austin clicked off the call and entered his office.

He found Izzy sitting at his desk with Névé lying in her doggie bed. The sight warmed his heart. *I could get used to this.*

Stop. Focus. Remember your vow.

After Clara's death, Izzy and Austin's friendship had fizzled. Austin guessed she blamed him for his mistake that night. He spent long hours talking to his adoptive parents and decided being a police officer wasn't for him. He agreed to stay at the ranch and learn the ropes, so he tendered his resignation to Chief Constable Tremblay. Izzy's father had tried to talk him out of it, but Austin had made his decision. There was no going back.

He couldn't take the silence with Izzy. He was about to tell her his true feelings for her, but after that night, he clammed up. They'd never have a relationship because of what he did. After a year had passed, he tried to get into the dating game but no one measured up to his Izzy. Every girl he dated broke it off within weeks, claiming his lack of attention to them was evidence that he had baggage. They weren't wrong.

He was unworthy of love. His biological parents had proven that to him when they gave him up for adoption. They didn't want him.

And neither did any woman.

So he'd vowed to himself to focus on the ranch, and talked his father into starting a K-9 training facility. Two years into his K-9 training business, his parents had died in a horrible car accident along the Rocky Mountains. Austin had been heartbroken and thrust himself further into ranching and training dogs.

And never gave another thought to policing.

Until now.

He wanted to keep Izzy safe and help her solve this case. Even if that meant putting himself in danger.

Could he stay objective and not allow his rising feelings for this woman overpower him?

You've got this, Austin.

He mustered strength and approached his desk. "You look good sitting here."

Wait, did he just really say that?

He cleared his throat. "I mean, you look comfy." He was a bumbling fool. *Get it together, Murray.*

She smiled and picked up a picture of Austin with his father. "I've always loved this picture of you two. This was taken when you first joined HRPD, right?"

"Excellent memory."

She huffed and placed the photo back down. "Apparently, not always."

"It will come. We just need to help it along." Austin opened a closet and brought out his rolling whiteboard. "Add your pictures to this. I use it for planning training routines for the dogs." He pushed it in between the two desks.

"Perfect." Izzy spread out the pictures from the file folder Doug had left on the opposite desk. "Let's start by adding these to the board."

"Are Rebecca and Blaire okay?" Austin lifted the tape out from his desk drawer and handed it to her.

"They are. Blaire yelled at me for putting them in a state of panic, but I had to warn them."

"Sorry. Doug is sending a patrol car." Austin eyed the photos. "Okay, where do you want to start?"

"Don't you have work to do?"

"Sawyer and the ranch hands can handle it." He picked up a picture. "How well did you know your father's CI?"

"I barely knew Sims. Dad referred to him often, but never by name. Said he was reliable. I found his name and number on the inside cover of Dad's journal." She broke off a piece of tape and added the pictures one by one.

Austin picked up a black marker and wrote the name Padilla at the top of the board, then a question mark below it. "Did your father ever mention this name?"

"No. I remember everything before the cyberattack at the station." She picked up a red marker and wrote *Drug Lord* beneath his name, then *bath salts*. "We know he—or she—is selling this form of drugs."

"How do you know that?"

"That information was in Dad's journal, just not the name Padilla." She tapped the marker on her chin. "Maybe he didn't know."

She drew a line beneath Padilla and wrote Ned Bolton's name beside it, connecting the two.

"Or didn't want to record the name. Do you think Ned was just a thug or a dealer under Padilla?"

"Good question. I got the impression he was only an enforcer."

"Yeah, he didn't seem the salesman type." Austin wrote *thumb drive* to the right of the pictures. "Okay, we know from your interview with him that Ned said you had a thumb drive. Any ideas of where you would have hidden it?"

Izzy paced the spacious office.

Her thinking mode.

She stopped at the window and turned. "I'm drawing a blank."

"Be patient. It will come. I just know it." Austin's radio squawked, and he unhooked it from his belt. "Go ahead."

"Perimeter is secure."

"Thanks, Sawyer." Austin checked his watch. "It's getting late and we haven't eaten all day. Time to start supper?"

"On it. Heading to the kitchen now."

Austin set the radio on his desk. "Anything else you want to add before we break for supper?"

Izzy set the marker on the board's ledge. "I hate not being able to remember. It's so unusual—and hard."

"Welcome to my world." Austin plunked into his desk chair. "You're trying too—"

Izzy snapped her fingers. "Wait. I want to go to my condo. I must have hidden the drive somewhere there."

"That's not wise, Iz. Your place is probably being closely watched by Padilla and his men." How could Austin convince her it wasn't safe?

"I have to, Austin. I have to try to help jog my memory."

Austin pushed himself upright. "If Chief Constable Halt finds out, he won't be happy."

"I don't care." Her raised voice caused Névé to hop up on all fours and bark.

"Névé, silence," Austin commanded.

The dog whimpered but obeyed.

"I'm sorry, Austin, but I need to find out the truth. With or without your help." She flew out of the room.

Austin squatted in front of his malamute. "Sorry, girl. She's just on edge."

How could Austin keep his ex-partner safe when she wouldn't listen to reason?

Izzy was tired of people telling her what to do and what not to do. First Blaire, then Austin. *Get it together, Iz. It's not their fault. They're only trying to protect you.*

Well, with Blaire, she wasn't so sure. She and her sister had been at odds for a while now. Why, Izzy didn't know. She had confronted her younger sister, but Blaire wouldn't give her a reason. Only that she was tired of having to live in her sister's shadow.

What exactly did that mean? Blaire was smart, beautiful and everyone loved her. Izzy, on the other hand, had butted heads with some. Could it be because of Izzy's perfect memory? Was her sister still jealous of that after all these years?

Sometimes Izzy wished it was her sister who had hyperthymesia and not her. It had been both a blessing and a curse all these years. Right now, it was creating havoc not being able to remember.

Lord, if You're listening, please show me what happened in those three hours. I feel it's vital to Dad's case. Protect my family. Help soften Blaire's heart toward me. I want my sister back.

Her cell phone trilled, and she swiped the screen. Doug. She hit answer and entered the country-style dining room. Table and chairs, along with furnishings made from logs, adorned the spacious area. "Hey, partner. You have good news?"

"Not much. Nothing on the cell phone, and the video footage from the station was wiped clean. We determined where the hack came from, though."

"Where?" Izzy plunked down at the table.

"Fisher confessed to clicking the link, but they spoofed the IP address to mimic yours. However, digital forensics traced it to a company called King & Sons." Tapping on a keyboard could be heard through the phone. "We can't find much on it and are wondering if it's a shell corporation."

Izzy ran her fingers along the smooth wood plank table, admiring the finishing. "Let me look into it from here."

"The digital team can handle it, Izzy."

"Doug, you know my hacking skills, and it's driving me nuts to not do anything."

Doug harrumphed. "I know I can't stop you, but please be careful."

She stood and sauntered to the large bay window, peering out into the backyard.

Sawyer entered the barn, leading his horse into the stable.

Wait. Izzy froze.

Sawyer's last name was King. Was there a connection? Probably a stretch, but how well did Austin know his ranch foreman? "I'm doing this, Doug. I need to know who King & Sons are."

If not for the case's sake, but for Austin's.

He could have a wolf among his dogs.

"I know your skills and I'm not stopping you." Doug was silent for a moment. "Izzy, Austin told me about your plans to go to your condo. Stay away."

Izzy banged her palm on the wall beside the window. *Tattletale.* "I may have hidden the drive there, Doug. I have to go."

"When are you going?"

"In the morning." *And I need to convince Austin to take me.*

"I'll have someone patrol the area overnight. Just to be on the safe side."

"Good, thanks, bud. You're the best. What would I do without you?"

He chuckled. "You'd be lost. Have a good evening and stay safe. I'll touch base in the morning. Don't leave the ranch until you hear from me. Got it?"

She saluted, even though he couldn't see her. "Yes, boss. Night." She ended the call.

A crash resonated from the kitchen area.

Woof!

"Hey, girl, let's go find Austin. He has some explaining to do." Izzy marched across the hall to the kitchen with Névé at her heels, then halted at a full stop.

Austin was drenched in white powder.

A broken bag of flour lay on the floor.

"Stay back. I need to sweep up the mess." Austin puffed a cloud of white from his mouth.

How could she stay mad at the handsome rancher when his face was covered with flour?

Her hand flew to her mouth to conceal the laughter wanting to escape.

"Go ahead. Laugh. I'm sure I look a fright."

She giggled. "What were you planning on making with the flour?"

He wiped his face with a dish towel. "Biscuits."

Izzy walked to the narrow door. "If memory serves me correctly, the broom is in here." She opened the door and brought it out.

"Thanks. Be careful not to slip."

Izzy tiptoed to where the mess lay and swept. "Austin, why did you tell Doug about me wanting to go to the condo?"

"Thought he should know." He snatched the dish cloth and wiped the counter. "Besides, he asked me to keep him informed."

Her neck muscles corded. "I was going to tell him. I can take care of myself, you know. Or did you forget that?"

"Of course not, Iz. But you're under my roof, and it's my responsibility to keep you safe."

Cool your jets, Izzy. He's not the enemy. "I'm sorry. I know you're only trying to help."

"God brought you back into my life for a reason."

"God? I think He forgot about me." She finished sweeping and grabbed the dustpan.

"Why would you say that? I thought you believed."

"I do—well, I did. Until He stopped showing me His plan for my life."

Austin took the dustpan from her hand. "I understand. It's hard to see God's journey for us when we can't even see around the bend in front of us. He knows the big picture." Austin placed the pan near a pile of flour.

She stopped sweeping. "When did you get so profound in your thinking?"

"Let's just say I've been digging into God's word more during the past ten years."

"I'm impressed." She swept the rest of the flour into the dustpan.

"So, you're not upset with me anymore?"

"Hard to stay mad at you, especially with flour on your face." She reached up and wiped a spot from his cheek, lingering a little longer than she should.

Their gazes held, silence booming in the spacious kitchen. Emotions wrestled inside Izzy, and she struggled to contain them.

What are you thinking, Austin?

Questions flooded Izzy's mind. How could her feelings from ten years ago return in such a short period? Did he feel the same? Why did he freeze that day?

The front door slammed.

Austin cleared his throat and stepped away, breaking the awkward moment. "That's Sawyer. He's making supper for us after he cleans up."

"Austin, how well do you know Sawyer? Do you trust him?"

"Completely." He emptied the flour into the garbage can. "Why would you ask that?"

How much should she tell him? "Doug mentioned the team traced the station's hack to a company called King & Sons."

"Come on, Iz. King is a popular last name."

Doubts crawled over Izzy's arms like an inchworm, sending chills exploding throughout her body as a question rose.

Could Austin be unbiased when it came to his best friend?

SIX

While sipping coffee, Austin studied Izzy's evidence board the next morning to piece together what happened during her attack. Frustration corded his muscles over the fact that she could have died. Thankfully, he and Doug had arrived when they did. Their presence had scared off the suspects.

Izzy had added *King & Sons* to the whiteboard under Padilla's name with a question mark. Austin clenched his jaw. Did she really think Sawyer could be part of this illegal drug ring? There were many King families across the province. When Izzy had asked Sawyer at the supper table how many were in his family, Sawyer said he was an only child.

"Morning, bud." Sawyer moved beside him, coffee in hand. "What's all this?"

"Izzy's evidence board. We're trying to piece together what happened during that three hours she can't remember."

Sawyer sipped his coffee. "I wanted to mention something. Had a rough day yesterday with the ranch hands."

Austin's neck muscles tensed. "Do I need to intervene? Be the bad guy? I can."

Sawyer chuckled. "Oh, I know. I've seen that streak. No, just some issues with the new younger guy, but I've got it under control. Laid down the law of the land, so to speak."

"How's Maverick doing?"

They had hired Maverick quickly after they lost an employee to another ranch on the other side of Harturn River. Austin had presumed the man was fitting in perfectly. Perhaps that had been an incorrect assumption.

"Just a few incidents with two other hands. I nipped it in the bud yesterday. I hope." Sawyer approached the board and tapped on Ned Bolton's picture. "Wait, Ned and I went to school together. Why's he on here?"

"He attacked me." Izzy entered the room with Névé at her heels. She massaged the bruise on her face. "Did this to me."

Sawyer winced. "Ned did that to you? So sorry."

"Sure did. How well did you know him?"

Sawyer rubbed his temple. "We hung out together for a bit, then he got in with the wrong crowd. Was suspended from school for fighting. Never saw him again after that."

"I guess he got his nickname of Scrapper honestly." Izzy walked to the board and wrote *Scrapper* beside Ned's name.

Sawyer turned to Austin. "Time to round up the dogs. You in?"

"Austin, before you answer that, Doug just called. He gave my condo the all-clear, so I wanted to go over there now." Her eyes shifted to Sawyer. "If I can steal him away for a few hours."

Sawyer shrugged. "Fine by me. I'll grab Maverick. I want to introduce him to the dog training aspect of the ranch. Izzy, are you sure you should be leaving? It's not safe."

Austin finished his coffee. "I'll be with her, and I'll take a couple of dogs with us."

Névé barked.

Austin leaned over and ruffled the dog's ears. "Of course you can come."

"Be careful you two." Sawyer walked to the entranceway and turned. "Take your own personal SUV, Austin. We don't want to advertise the ranch if you take the K-9 vehicle. They may be watching her condo." He left the room.

Austin bristled. "He's right, but first you need breakfast, Iz." He touched the small of her back, nudging her toward the door. "Go."

Fifty minutes later Austin parked along the side of Izzy's street a few houses down from her condo. Turning off the engine, he shifted in his seat to face her. "Okay, we'll walk from here and pretend we're out for a stroll with our dogs. You take Névé and I'll take Goose."

"Got it." She climbed from the SUV.

Austin shook his head. "But wait for me to leave first. Iz, you haven't changed." He pursed his lips and got out of his vehicle, hustling around to the rear. He opened the back and let the dogs out.

He passed Névé's leash to Izzy. "Remember, easy stroll."

"Got it, Austin. Let's go, girl." Izzy and the malamute trudged through the snowbank and onto the sidewalk.

Austin and Goose followed. "Beautiful day for a walk, right?"

"Sure is, hon." Izzy winked.

He loved that she played along with their charade and he wasn't wrong. The sun provided not only warmth but added to their cover. Perfect day for a romantic stroll.

If only that was the truth.

As they approached Izzy's condo, Austin tugged at her arm. "Wait here with Névé. Goose and I will check things out before you go any farther. I realize Doug said it was clear, but that was earlier this morning. I'll whistle when it's safe. You remember the signal I used to give while we were on calls?"

"Of course. One long whistle means it's safe. Two short equals danger. Got it." She positioned herself beside a tree. "Girl, wanna play in the snow?"

Névé barked.

"Of course you do." Izzy scooped snow and tossed it to the malamute.

She launched into the air and caught it in her mouth.

Austin longed to stay and play with the duo. Perhaps start a snowball fight, but he and Goose had a job to do. He'd trained the German shepherd not only in scents but in protection. "Let's go, bud."

After walking around the block of Izzy's condo, Goose and Austin perused the property. The shepherd hadn't alerted to anything, so Austin let out one long whistle.

A couple moments later Izzy appeared with Névé at her heels and smothered in snow.

Austin chuckled. "Did you dunk my dog in the snow?"

"Nope. Just wrestled with her. She's a good girl."

"That she is." He gestured toward her detached condo's door. "Wanna go in the front or back?"

"Back. Some of my neighbors are nosy."

"That's why I love the country."

The group slogged through the snow and Austin turned as they rounded the corner, checking for any spying eyes. However, the neighborhood was silent.

Good.

He followed Izzy up the back steps.

She inserted her key and pushed open the door. "Let's get in quickly before Ezra sees us."

"I remember him. He still lives behind you?"

"Yup." They stepped into the back entryway.

Goose growled.

Névé barked.

Austin stiffened. Not good.

His dogs were alerting to something or someone inside the house.

Izzy's pulse skyrocketed, sending her adrenaline racing through her body and into a panicked state. *Breathe, Izzy. Remember, you're a cop and should be used to danger.* But it was different when that danger was in her own home. She reached for her sidearm, only to realize it wasn't on her hip. She was off duty. Izzy hurried to her deacon's bench and took out a tactical flashlight she kept there for emergencies. She lifted it as a weapon.

Névé nudged her legs as if guarding her from harm.

Austin lowered Izzy's arm. "Iz, let Goose go first. He's also trained in protection."

"I am too."

"I know that. Just let Goose do his job. We don't even know if there is anyone inside." Austin unleashed the shepherd. "Seek!"

The dog bounded down the hallway into the front of the

house. His nails clicked on the floors as Izzy pictured him moving from room to room.

After what seemed like an hour, Goose returned to their location, barked, then glanced backward.

"What does that mean?" Izzy once again raised the flashlight.

"He's found something, but isn't alerting to danger." Austin snatched the flashlight from her hand. "Let me go first."

"Wait, who's the cop here?" She smirked. "Trying to be the hero?"

"Nope, just a gentleman." Austin addressed his dog. "What did you find, boy?"

Goose barked, trotted down the hall and turned from the living room entryway.

"He's telling us to follow. Névé, heel." Austin moved toward Goose.

Izzy followed with the malamute at her side and stepped into her living room.

And halted in her tracks.

Her furniture, bookshelf and end table drawers were all overturned. Books lay everywhere. The perp had cut open her couch cushions.

Not good.

Someone had invaded her home.

Izzy balled her fists as anger replaced the panic consuming her earlier. "Ugh! Someone was looking for the flash drive, and I don't know if they would have found it because I don't remember where I put it." Her heightened tone boomed in the room.

Névé barked at Izzy's tempered statement.

"Sorry, girl." Izzy rubbed the dog's ears.

Once again, Goose barked and trotted toward Izzy's office.

"There's more." Austin took out his cell phone and followed Goose, peeking into the room. "It's a mess too. I'm calling Doug. Izzy, we need to get out of the house and not touch anything." He punched buttons and positioned his phone to his ear.

Izzy realized they had to vacate the premises, but she wanted to see her favorite spot in the condo—her office and reading room.

Austin's conversation with Doug morphed into the background in a tunnellike effect as Izzy marched to her office but remained in the doorway. They had pulled out her desk drawers, and their contents littered the floor. Slashed paintings lay ruined. Every one of them.

Izzy's hand flew to her mouth. *How could someone do this?* Now she understood how it felt to be on the other end of that proverbial stick. A tear rolled down her right cheek, followed by another.

Hands grasped her shoulders from behind, and she jumped.

"Sorry, Iz. Just didn't want you to go any farther into the room. Doug is on his way with forensics."

Austin turned her around before she could rid herself of the tears streaming down her face.

He wiped them away with his thumbs. "I'm sorry. I know this is your favorite room, and it violates your privacy."

"My dad gave most of these paintings to me. Now they're ruined. Every one of them." She fell into his arms and sobbed.

Austin's hold tightened around her body.

Névé whimpered from the hallway.

"She wants to console you too, but we need to get out of the house." He took her hand and led her toward the rear entrance. "Once forensics is done, we'll go back in and try to figure things out. Okay?"

She nodded and let him guide her outside. The cold stung her face, bringing her out of the stupor holding her captive. Izzy yanked her hand away and plunked down on the bottom step. "Whoever did this won't get away with it. Mark my words, I *will* find those responsible. They will pay."

Sirens filtered through the streets.

"Howdy, neighbor!" Ezra's head popped up over the fence, peering into her backyard.

Great, he was all she needed right now. "Hey, Ezra."

"What's going on and who are these dogs? I hate dogs. Theys ain't goin' to bark constantly, are they?"

Izzy pushed herself up. "Don't worry, Ezra. They're not staying."

Clouds moved in, blocking the sun and darkening the region along with Izzy's mood.

The sirens screamed louder, indicating Doug and his team were almost there.

"Them coppers coming here?" Ezra clucked his tongue. "This neighborhood is goin' to the dogs."

Izzy ignored his obvious intentional pun. She might as well tell him, as he'd find out anyway. "Had a break-in, Ezra. Don't worry. Your house is fine."

"Did you see anything suspicious, sir?" Austin approached the sixtysomething man.

"Did not and if there were burglars, I would have seen them." He tapped his temple. "Nothing gets by these eyes."

Well, apparently they did. Izzy zipped her coat up farther, attempting to ward off the chill and her foul mood.

A car door slammed.

"Officers will probably ask you questions, Ezra. Catch ya later." Izzy waved before turning to Austin. "Doug's here. Let's go."

After Izzy had a walk with Austin and the dogs and visited a coffee shop, Doug allowed them to enter the condo. Snow had changed the previous sunny sky into a darkened, ominous one, and blanketed the area once again and created havoc.

Izzy stomped snow from her boots as she walked up the steps and entered her trashed home. "It's coming down hard."

"Already have accident reports coming in." Doug turned from her living room fireplace. "I started the gas fireplace to take the chill off."

Izzy whipped off her hat, gloves and coat, throwing them into her closet. She positioned herself with her hands out in front of the fire. "Thanks. So much for a beautiful day."

Austin joined her, followed by the dogs. He pointed to a corner not touched by vandalism. "Lay down."

The K-9s obeyed.

"Now that forensics is finished, I want you to give me your statement." Doug brought out his notebook. "Tell me what happened. Was anything stolen?"

"I don't think so." Izzy recounted their steps in explicit detail from the time they arrived to when they backed out of her condo. She itemized every trashed object as she pictured the scene in her head. "Now, we didn't go upstairs or check the other rooms. I assume they struck there too?"

"I'm afraid so. Do you think they were looking for this supposed flash drive you hid?"

"Don't you, Doug? Did any officers canvass the area for other B and Es?"

"Yes, and nothing surfaced. Apparently, one neighbor behind you had lots to say about our police force helping the area go to the dogs."

"Ezra. He's quite the handful." Izzy rubbed her hands together, hoping to speed up the warming process. "I want to look through the house now. See if it sparks any memories of where I hid that drive."

"Yeah, I'm guessing from the trail of carnage the burglars left, they didn't find it." Doug rubbed his brow. "Sorry, Izzy. When I patrolled earlier, there were no indications someone had broken in. No footprints. Nothing."

Austin picked up a ripped cushion. "So, they must have just been here. Do you think they're watching the house? I did a sweep and saw nothing suspicious. I thought the footprints were yours checking out the place."

"I have units patrolling again now." He tucked his notebook away. "I have to go do the paperwork."

"Where are you working from since the station is under repair?" Izzy squatted by a drawer and lifted it, replacing the coasters back inside.

"For now, in the library. Not the ideal spot, and Halt is antsy to get back into our building. However, it won't be for a few weeks." Doug walked to the front door. "You okay here by yourself?"

Were they? Izzy prayed they would be. "We'll be fine. Can you send a unit to Mom's and check on them?"

"Will do. I'll give you an update later. Tell me if you find the drive." Doug left the condo.

"Where do you want to start?" Austin righted an overturned chair.

Izzy stood and tapped her chin. "I'll do a cursory look through the rooms and then decide."

She spent the next few minutes moving from room to room with Névé at her heels. Seemed the malamute wasn't leaving her side. Not that Izzy minded. She had fallen in love with the sweet animal.

Izzy approached her office. "Should I start here, girl?"

Névé barked.

"She agrees." Austin entered the room and picked up a painting. "I remember this one."

Tears threatened to spill, but Izzy willed them back. "Dad painted that one of his old homestead. Lots of memories there. Blaire and I used to pretend we were princesses on a quest. We made swords out of branches and ran through the fields."

"How's she doing?"

Izzy let out a long sigh. "She hasn't been herself lately."

"Guy problems?"

She raised her hands, palms up. "Not sure. She hasn't dated since the last one broke her heart." Izzy didn't want to talk about dating.

Sitting at her desk, she scanned the room slowly, looking for any signs of possible stolen items.

But nothing came to mind.

"Anything missing?"

She shook her head.

"Do you think you would have hidden it in here?" Austin propped the painting against the wall.

"Wish I could remember, but nothing is coming to me." She drummed her nails on the desk. *Izzy, if you were to hide a thumb drive, where would you put it?*

An open box caught her attention. She had packed up her father's things from his office at HRPD and brought them here, intending to take them to her mother, but hadn't.

The lid leaned on its side against the cardboard box. The perp had looked inside.

Her breath caught. Something about the box drew her like a butterfly to its favorite flower. She pushed herself up and brought it to her desk.

She rummaged through the contents. Her father's books, nameplate, pen set, spring jacket, and...

Her fingers stopped when she grazed a metal object—his challenge coin. Why wasn't it in its velvet pouch? She lifted it from the box and examined the engraving.

Izzy's grandfather had given it to his son when he first became a police officer.

Stay safe, son. Always come home to your family.

It was what Hezekiah Tremblay said to his son and then later to his granddaughter when Izzy joined the force.

Chief Constable Justin Tremblay always carried it in his pocket. Or at least Izzy thought that. She had found it in his desk drawer the day after he died. *Why didn't you have it in your pocket?*

Not that she believed the coin held a secret to staying safe, but her father always had it on him, rolling it between his knuckles. Just like that famous pirate from the movies.

She sat straighter as a memory flashed.

Her removing the coin from the green pouch before heading out her back door.

She sprang to her feet.

Austin turned from picking up her books. "What is it?"

She held up the coin. "I think I put the flash drive in my dad's challenge coin pouch before going outside."

"What does that mean?"

She winced. "I believe I hid it in the backyard."

The recent snowfall may have buried the pouch. How would they ever find it?

"Do you have any idea where you think you would have hidden it? A special spot in your yard?" Austin took the coin from her fingers and examined the object. A roaring lion was etched on one side. He flipped it over. *Be strong and of a good courage. Joshua 1:9.* "I love this verse."

"So did Dad." Her face twisted in confusion. "No, I don't know where I put it." She fisted her palms and banged on her desk.

Névé and Goose hopped to their feet, ready for action.

"Is this memory lapse what most people have to deal with?" Izzy raked her hand through her shoulder-length brown waves. "I'm not used to feeling this frustrated over memories."

Austin chuckled. "Welcome to everyone else's life." When she didn't respond, Austin rubbed her arm. "Sorry, not trying to make light of your situation. I know this is frustrating."

"It's just the unknown and I hate the unknown." She chewed on her lip. "It's why I'm struggling with God right now. He seems to have hidden His path for me."

There was a story behind her words. What was it? "What's made you feel that way?"

Not that Austin didn't question God and His direction for Austin's life.

"Never mind." She eyed the malamute. "Wait, isn't Névé a search and rescue dog?"

"Yes, but for *humans*, Iz. Too bad we don't have a human scent we could try." Austin handed the coin back to her. "It's okay, Iz. It will come."

Her eyes brightened. She pointed to a jacket. "That's my father's. His scent would probably still be on it and the pouch, right? The box has remained closed over the last two weeks."

Austin lifted it out of the box. "It's a long shot, but worth trying. Are you sure it's probably in the backyard?"

"My flash of memory revealed me pulling the strings to close the pouch and grabbing my jacket. I went out the back door. Not sure what it means and that's all I remember."

"Well, let's go then." Austin turned to the dogs. "Come."

Once Austin and Izzy put on their coats, the group exited through the back door.

The wind bit Austin's face, and he drew in a breath. The sun had disappeared behind dark clouds, bringing an ominous feeling seeping into his bones.

"Let's get my girl working before the wind picks up even more." Austin turned to Goose. "Goose, guard."

The shepherd lifted his nose in the air and advanced to the edge of the condo.

"Wait, isn't Goose a scent dog? Couldn't he help too?" Izzy stuffed on her hat.

"He is, but Névé is better, and I want Goose protecting us in case those assailants are watching." Austin squatted in front of his malamute and raised the jacket to her nose.

She sniffed the clothing.

"Névé, track!"

She lifted her snout and sniffed the air before moving throughout the backyard, stopping to stick her nose in the snow. She sniffed along a two-foot tree stump holding a birdhouse, then over to the fence, then back to the stump.

"Is she confused?"

"No, she's making sure she has the scent correct." Austin observed his dog as she circled the stump, then sat. "She's found something."

They trudged through the snow toward the birdhouse.

Austin removed a treat from his cargo pants pocket. "Good girl." He ruffled her ears and tossed her the treat.

"So, she's alerted to something in either the stump or the birdhouse." Izzy ran her gloved hand along the stump, squatting to get into the low area.

Austin did the same to the birdhouse. "Is there something special about this feeder?"

"Only that my dad made it for me." She sprang up. "Wait, it's weathered throughout the years and I noticed a hole starting near the bottom."

Austin moved beside her.

She took off her gloves and threw them on the ground before sticking her index finger in the hole, then drew in a sharp breath.

"What is it?"

She edged her middle finger in the opening and pulled out a green velvet pouch. "Yes! Good job, Névé."

The malamute barked.

Izzy opened the pouch and dropped the contents into her palm.

A tiny flash drive.

Behind them, Goose barked.

Austin froze.

His other dog was alerting to danger.

Névé also growled.

Pfft. Pfft.

Bullets hit the stump.

Snow sprayed at their feet.

Goose barked again and barreled toward the shots.

Névé pounced on top of Izzy, knocking her to the ground.

"Get behind the stump!" Austin dropped beside Izzy and Névé, nudging them around their only means of cover. His gaze darted back and forth in search of the shooter.

They were right. The suspects had been watching from a distance and were just waiting for the right time to strike.

And he had no weapon to protect them.

SEVEN

Izzy's heartbeat jackhammered like a rabbit when cornered by an enemy with nowhere to run. *Lord, protect us. We're defenseless.* She stuffed the drive and pouch into her coat pocket, then wrapped a protective arm around Névé and waited for more shots, praying they wouldn't reach them.

But no further gunfire erupted.

The dog snuggled into Izzy as they ducked behind the thick stump. She eased her head around the side. "Can you see anyone?"

Barking sounded in the distance.

"No, stay back. Goose is searching."

Approaching sirens returned to the neighborhood.

"Good, I'm guessing Ezra called it in. For once, I appreciate his nosiness." Izzy hauled out her cell phone and hit her partner's number. "Calling Doug."

"Izzy, we're out front now. What's going on?"

She put him on speaker. "Doug, shots fired. We're pinned behind the stump in the backyard. I think the shooter is gone."

Goose continued to bark.

Austin inched closer to the phone. "Doug, follow Goose's barking. He's alerted to something."

"Copy. I'm sending Fisher around back to you." A car door slammed.

Movement sounded, and Izzy peeked out.

Fisher stood in a protective stance with his weapon raised. "Stay put. I don't want you guys catching stray bullets. Carver will give the all-clear once the others have secured the area."

"Got it." Izzy wanted to join her colleagues but couldn't. If she tried, she knew Fisher would probably report her to Halt. Izzy respected Fisher's great police work, but they didn't always see eye to eye on some aspects of a situation.

Austin leaned closer. "You still have the drive?"

"In my pocket."

"Good, I was scared you dropped it in the snow when Névé tackled you." He rubbed the dog's back. "Good girl for protecting Izzy."

Woof!

Fisher's radio crackled, and Doug's voice sailed over the airwaves. "Get Austin here. Suspects are gone, but his dog is alerting to something and won't move."

Izzy and Austin rose to their feet.

"On my way." Austin plodded through the snow toward Goose's barking.

Izzy scooped up her gloves and put them back on, then followed with Névé by her side. "Fisher, stay here in case they circle back."

"Tremblay, this isn't my first rodeo."

Oops. Izzy, stay out of it. You're not on duty. "Sorry, I know." She patted his shoulder and continued after Austin.

Moments later they arrived at the edge of the tree line at the end of Izzy's street. Goose paced, barking into the woods.

"Goose, out!" Austin commanded.

The dog obeyed and sat.

Izzy approached Doug. "Thanks for getting here so quickly."

"You okay?" Doug kept his eyes trained on the forest with his gun raised.

"Yes. Any sign of the shooter?"

"None, but I'm wondering if they're hiding in the woods. Austin, thoughts on what your dog is alerting to?"

"He's definitely agitated about something." Austin looked down the street. "You have any other officers that could join me? I'll get Goose to track into the woods, but I don't want to go in unarmed."

"We're down a few men right now." Doug's radio crackled.

"Carver, movement spotted near Tremblay's condo." Fisher's breathless voice revealed he was running.

Once again, Goose growled.

Névé joined him.

Something or someone was agitating the dogs.

"Doug, I know you have permission to carry a secondary weapon. Can I have it?" Izzy stuck out her hand. "I'll go with Austin. You join Fisher."

"Are you trying to get me into trouble? You're off duty."

"I know, but what choice do we have?" She tilted her head. "It's not like you're giving a gun to a civilian."

He shook his head and took out his secondary gun from his ankle holster. "Don't make me regret this decision." He handed it to her.

"I've got this. Go." Izzy pointed back toward her condo.

Doug jogged down the street.

"How do you want to do this, Iz?"

She checked the gun before raising it. "I'll go first. Then we'll let the dogs do their thing." Izzy didn't wait for a response but advanced as quickly through the snow as she could, entering the woods. She stopped and surveyed her surroundings, listening for movement. The darkened clouds and snowstorm reduced the visibility, making it difficult to see anything in the dense forest.

A chickadee trilled from its perch above their heads. A jay squawked in return as if warning their friends of predators who've entered their forest.

"Slow down, Iz." Austin caught up to her. "Remember your partners."

"You're not my—"

Goose growled.

A shadow passed in between trees in front of them deeper into the forest.

Izzy raised her weapon. "Police, show yourself!"

The figure darted behind a Douglas fir.

"Goose, track!" Austin commanded.

The shepherd bounded through the snow toward the lurking suspect.

If it was a suspect. But who else would be in the forest hiding in the dead of winter and not answer her command?

"Give it up. You're surrounded." Izzy inched closer to where she'd last seen the person with Névé by her side. Seemed the malamute wasn't letting her go anywhere by herself.

Goose dashed toward a cluster of firs, then sat and barked ferociously.

"He's got something." Austin quickened his pace.

Izzy rushed by him. "Let me go first. I'm armed."

"Yes, but I also have a German shepherd ready to attack at my command." He moved a branch from her path. "We do it together."

She couldn't argue. Goose had already proven his worth. However, Austin's hesitation from years ago crept into her memory. Would he freeze like he had back then?

Trust, Izzy. Trust.

Her father's simple mantra played in her head like a skipping record. Why had it come to mind now?

Because the chief constable had believed in Austin's instincts even after he knew about what had happened that night. He had always given Austin the benefit of the doubt.

She didn't like it, but her father was right. Izzy nodded.

They proceeded toward the barking German shepherd.

Moments later they came upon the object of the dog's angered growl.

A man wearing a balaclava, waving a knife. "Get him away from me!"

"I trained this dog to attack to protect those around him." Austin stepped beside Goose.

"Drop your weapon." Izzy inched closer.

"You think I'm dumb? I do that and I'm a dead man."

Izzy searched her memory bank for voice recognition, but none came. She did not know this person. "We can protect you. Tell us why you ransacked my house."

"He'll kill me and my family. And yours." He lifted the knife higher.

"Who are you talking about?"

"Padilla."

"Who is this Padilla?" Wait, if this man only had a knife. Who shot at them? "Is Padilla nearby?"

Silence.

Austin gestured toward Goose. "Tell us or I'll command him to attack."

The man's cell phone rang. "That's him. If I don't answer, he'll kill us all."

"Why would you say that?" Izzy took another step closer.

"Because he's watching." He lifted his chin at something behind them.

Izzy whirled around, looking in the direction they had just come.

Névé growled. She had also seen what Izzy did.

A figure dressed in black from head to toe stood pointing a rifle at them.

A memory flashed.

The same shadowy figure lurking in the dark alleyway.

"Who are you?" Izzy yelled.

The phone continued to ring.

The man pointed to his ear.

Izzy turned back around and spoke to the suspect. "Put it on speaker."

He hit the button. "We're here, boss."

"Constable Tremblay, nice to see you again." The menacing, distorted voice sailed through the speaker.

"Who are you and what do you want?" Izzy turned back toward the figure standing in the distance.

"I think you know. Lower your weapon." He paused. "The flash drive for your sister's life."

"What makes you think I have this supposed drive?" Would he call her bluff?

She had to contact Doug to get reinforcements here, but had no radio. Could she somehow get her fingers to tap her SOS feature on her cell phone?

"I saw you pull it out from the birdhouse." He tapped the scope on his rifle, then shifted the weapon toward Austin. "Do it or he dies."

The perp in front of them held out his hand. "He's gonna kill us all, man. Hand it over."

Izzy sucked in a ragged breath.

"Don't do it, Iz." Austin looked at Goose, then Névé, then back to Izzy.

She knew him well enough to know he had a plan. A plan obviously involving his dogs. Could she trust him with her sister's life?

Trust, Izzy. Trust.

The mantra played again in her mind, and she dipped her chin in acknowledgment.

"Goose, Névé, get 'em!" Austin's whispered command spoke volumes as he gestured one arm toward the man with the knife and the other toward Padilla.

Goose leaped and seized the man's arm. The assailant cried out and dropped the knife.

Névé barreled through the snow in a zigzag fashion toward Padilla.

The combined effort was enough to distract the man in black.

Izzy lifted her weapon and squeezed the trigger, providing covering fire for Névé.

She wouldn't let Padilla shoot the dog she now loved.

Austin lunged at the man in front of them. "Goose, out!"

The German shepherd released his grip on the suspect's arm. Austin shoved the man's hands behind him, pinned him down and placed his knee on his back. With his right hand, Austin removed his cell and hit Doug's number.

"Austin, you guys okay? I just heard a shot."

"Got one suspect in custody. Izzy is in pursuit of Padilla. Send backup. Now!" Austin prayed they'd arrive before the drug lord got off more shots.

Névé barked.

Austin turned to check Izzy's bearings.

The man in black snaked through the trees, but stopped behind a large Douglas fir, taking aim once again.

Névé and Izzy needed help. Now. "Goose, protect and cover!"

The German shepherd rocketed through the snow toward Padilla in the same zigzag pattern the malamute had taken. It was how Austin trained his dogs when in a dangerous pursuit.

Thankfully Austin had trained the Alaskan malamute in the same fashion as he had his protection dogs—just in case.

Lord, keep them safe and bring help quickly.

"Izzy, he's taking aim. Névé, cover!" Austin prayed the command would also tell Izzy what to do.

She ducked behind a cluster of trees.

Another shot rang out, but the bullet flew wide, spraying the snow near Goose. The dog compensated and changed directions.

The suspect squirmed beneath Austin's hold.

Austin struggled with letting the man go, but Izzy needed help. *Trust.* The word came to him in a flash, and he knew the source. He had to trust in Izzy's abilities—and his dogs. God was in control. Wasn't He? Doubts still tended to seep into Austin's thoughts, especially lately.

He shoved his knee harder into the middle of his captive's spine. "You're not going anywhere, bud."

Loud voices entered the woods.

Good, help had arrived.

"Let me go or I'm a dead man."

"The police can protect you."

"You don't understand. Padilla's connections go deep. He has eyes everywhere." Once again, he squirmed.

"Tell me who he is and we can stop this."

The man cursed. "You can't."

Movement along the path caught Austin's attention. Doug and the others had appeared with their weapons raised. "Status report."

"Shooter passed that way," Izzy yelled, pointing north. "Austin has the other pinned down."

"You stay here in case he circles back. Get the suspect to Fisher. He's still at your condo watching." Doug and the additional constables pursued, trudging through the snow.

Izzy and his dogs returned to Austin's side. She stuffed the gun into the waistband at the small of her back and squatted in front of the suspect. "Has he said anything?"

"Only that no one can stop Padilla."

Goose and Névé flanked Izzy.

Izzy gestured toward them. "Have you met my friends here? I will stop Padilla."

"Your father couldn't."

Austin didn't miss Izzy's tortured expression. "Iz, let's get this guy to Fisher. You need to check on Blaire." He hauled the suspect to his feet, keeping a firm grip on him.

Her eyes widened, and she bolted upright. Izzy extracted her phone from her coat pocket, tapping on it before putting it up to her ear. "Pick up, Blaire."

Austin waited, holding his breath that Izzy's sister was okay and Padilla had only been bluffing. *Please make it so, Lord.*

"No answer." Izzy tapped her phone again. "Calling Mom as Blaire lives at Mom's place for now. She's a criminal profiler and has been working from home."

Seconds later Izzy brought the phone back down. "Austin, we need to get to Mom's. She's not answering either. Something isn't right."

"Let's go." Austin nudged his prisoner forward, addressing his dogs. "Come."

After getting an update from Doug that Padilla had disappeared, Austin drove to Rebecca Tremblay's house on a cul-de-sac near Harturn River's town limits. Izzy had returned the gun to Doug to do all the necessary paperwork involved in discharging a weapon. He promised to keep her updated once they interrogated the suspect. However, Austin doubted they'd get much more out of him than what they had. The thirtysomething had clammed up, stating he knew better than to rat out Padilla or his organization. Austin sensed the man really didn't know Padilla's identity anyway.

Izzy jumped out of the vehicle before Austin could cut the engine. "Wait for us, Iz. Ugh!" He exited the driver's side and jogged to the back to open the cages. "She's stubborn, isn't she? Névé, heel."

The malamute scampered to Izzy's side.

Austin attached Goose's leash. "Come, boy."

Izzy punched a code into the box on the wall and took out a key. She inserted it into the lock and thrust open the front door. "Mom! Blaire!"

So much for entering quietly. Seemed Izzy's concern for her family had trumped her protective police mode. "Izzy, wait up a second." Austin unleashed his German shepherd. "Goose, protect!"

The dog trotted in front of Izzy and Névé.

Austin yanked on Izzy's arm. "Are you trying to get yourself killed? Let Goose lead the way."

She clenched her hands into fists and pounded on her hips. "You're right. I let my emotions take over. I lost Dad. I can't lose Mom and Blaire, too."

Goose growled and whirled around, facing the front entrance, barking and baring his teeth.

"Izzy, what—"

Austin and Izzy pivoted.

Izzy's uncle stood in the doorway with his hands raised.

"Uncle Ford! What are you doing here?" Izzy thrust herself into his arms.

"Goose, out. Sit." Austin gave Névé a silent command to do the same.

The K-9s obeyed.

"What's going on? I got an SOS from your sister." Ford closed the door behind him. "She has me as a contact on her smartwatch."

Izzy clasped her uncle's arm. "I think the same people who got to Dad are after Mom and Blaire."

"You still think Justin was murdered?" Ford tilted his head, folding his arms across his chest. "I thought we settled this after his funeral. You need to let it rest."

"Sir, with everything that's happened in the past couple of days, Izzy was right about her father's death." Austin hated to get in the middle of family matters, but he didn't care for Ford's attitude.

The man inched closer and waggled his finger into Austin's face. "You stay out of it. This doesn't concern you."

Izzy lowered her uncle's arm. "Not true. He's given me refuge and saved me more than once. Tell me when Blaire sent the SOS."

He checked his phone. "About fifteen minutes ago. I got caught in traffic trying to get here and when I called, she didn't pick up." Ford raced down the corridor. "Rebecca, where are you?"

Pounding resonated upstairs.

"Mom?" Izzy took the steps two at a time.

Not again. "Goose, Névé, heel!" Austin flicked his hand toward Izzy.

The dogs bounded after her, along with Ford.

Austin followed.

Ford reached the top. "Rebecca, where are you? Blaire?"

The pounding increased along with muffled yells to the left.

"It's coming from Mom's room." Izzy dashed down the hallway.

The group entered the room.

A dresser blocked the walk-in closet door.

Someone had trapped Izzy's mom and sister inside.

Austin turned to Ford. "Help me move this."

They shoved the dresser to the right, and Izzy opened the door.

Her mother and sister scrambled to their feet. Their hands were bound behind them. They turned and stumbled from the room.

Izzy removed Rebecca's gag and untied her before bringing her into an embrace. "Are you okay?"

Ford approached Blaire and did the same. "Tell us what happened."

"The doorbell rang and when I opened the door, a masked man burst inside holding a gun. Then he—" Rebecca's sobs ended her account of the intrusion.

"I had my phone in my hand behind my back, so I quickly pressed the SOS button, hoping I could at least get Uncle Ford here." Blaire hurried to her mother's side and rubbed her arm.

"You did, but it must have only gone out to me as there are no police here." Ford brought his sister-in-law into his arms and caressed her back. "Shhhh…it's gonna be okay, Becky."

Austin noted the way Ford used Rebecca's nickname and how cozy he appeared to be with his brother's wife. Austin observed Izzy.

Her contorted expression told him she also noticed her uncle's intimate action. She took her mother's hand and guided her to a chair in the room's corner, breaking her uncle's hold. "Tell us what happened next."

"He took away our phones, then tied our hands and gagged us. Made us go upstairs and pushed us into the closet. We heard him moving the dresser in front of the door, so we realized we wouldn't be able to escape." Rebecca bit her lip. "Then everything silenced. It was like he just wanted to hide us."

Izzy spoke to Austin. "Padilla's way of telling me he's in control. We need to get Mom and Blaire into protective custody."

Austin's thoughts exactly, and he knew the perfect place for them to find refuge.

Murray K-9 Ranch.

He just had to beef up security first. Austin wouldn't let anything happen to the rest of Izzy's family.

Not on his watch.

EIGHT

Izzy adjusted the number of copies to two and hit the print button. She wasn't taking any chances this time around with her father's journal. She downloaded all the scanned pages from the drive and wanted a physical printout to add to her board. Visualizing every detail was how she worked and did her best thinking. She took an extra copy for safekeeping.

Névé slept on her mat placed in the room's corner. The dog's presence comforted her, but left her with a question. How would she say goodbye to this amazing animal when she solved her father's case and put those responsible behind bars?

And she *would* do that.

Austin had convinced Izzy's mother and Blaire to take refuge at his ranch. They had balked at the idea and Uncle Ford did too, but in the end, Izzy sold the idea as family time for bonding. Uncle Ford warned them he'd be checking in on them often. He didn't want his "girls" to be stressed by not being in their own place. He knew his sister-in-law well. Izzy's mother did not like change and losing her husband was huge. She had struggled ever since his death.

Izzy's father had done everything for her mother, even though she was highly capable. Spoiled by her husband, Rebecca Tremblay had gotten used to his pampering.

An image of Uncle Ford rubbing her mother's back popped into her mind. Izzy dug her fingernails into her palms. Why did his intimate touch bother her so much?

Because it's too soon.

Her father just passed. However, maybe the gesture was nothing. Uncle Ford was a kind, caring person and wanted to console his sister-in-law.

Concentrate. You have enough problems to deal with right now. Namely...getting those three hours back.

Izzy sighed and took the first printout from the tray, taping it to her evidence board. She placed the second copy in an envelope. She'd hide it in her room later.

Her cell phone buzzed in her back jeans pocket. She took it out and hit answer. "Tremblay here."

"Got something for you." Doug's voice filtered through the phone.

She put him on speaker and set her cell on the desk she'd commandeered. "I hope it's good news. I sure could use some."

"Everything okay?"

"Just tired and want the three-hour black hole to disappear." And she'd been struggling with having Austin so close. Not that she would admit that to Doug, but her past feelings resurfaced, and she had fought hard to stuff them away. Forever.

"It will come. So, we examined your mother's home, but didn't find any prints that weren't hers or Blaire's. The suspect most likely wore gloves." Rustling papers sounded through the speaker. "The perp you caught is Conroy Phillips. Has a past record of misdemeanors. Disturbing the peace, drunk driving, petty thefts. Nothing substantial. Until now."

Izzy wrote the name on a piece of paper. "Did you get anything from him?"

"Fisher and I cross-examined him hard. He's pretty tight-lipped, but he let two things slip. One was that Padilla's organization is far-reaching. Across Canada and even into Washington State."

"That makes sense, as it's right on the British Columbia border. Did he say anything about the drugs they're selling?"

"He only mentioned the bath salts, but we already knew about that."

"We need to find where they're producing the drugs and shut it down." Izzy sat on the corner of the desk and studied the board. "What was the other thing you discovered?"

"He let it slip that Padilla is close to finding where you're hidden."

Izzy's muscles locked, and she dropped her pen. It hit the desk and rolled onto the floor. "How? We've been so careful."

"But you haven't stayed put, Izzy. You need to stop leaving the safety of the ranch."

She hated being confined to one spot. The Tremblay blood in her prevented that from happening. "But I have to find the truth and get justice for Dad."

"I realize that, but stop putting yourself at risk. Let Fisher and I do the investigating."

How could she make him understand her need to bring her father's killer to justice? She had sensed her father's troubled mood before his death, but had failed to find out the cause. She'd been too busy with her own cases that she'd hadn't taken time to sit down with him and have a heart-to-heart.

And now it was too late.

Tears threatened to fall. She breathed in and out to stop them. *I miss you, Dad. Miss our chats. Why didn't I spend more time with you lately?*

"Izzy? You hear me?"

Doug's question ended her pity party.

"I did, and I'll be careful. I promise." However, she wouldn't promise not to leave the ranch again if her investigation warranted her to.

"Keep me apprised of your progress, as I know you will not stop." He chuckled. "Take care."

"You too." She clicked off the call.

She returned to printing the pages of her father's journal and adding them to the board.

"You're gonna need another board soon." Austin set a cup of coffee on her desk. "Here's some fuel for your afternoon."

"Thanks." She took a sip. "This is good. You still roast your own beans?"

"Of course. You know how much of a coffee snob I am." He

scooped up the fallen pen from the floor and set it beside her notebook, turning the page in his direction. "Who's Conroy Phillips?"

"The guy you caught in the woods." Izzy explained what information Doug had provided.

"Well, Sawyer and I have increased the ranch hands' awareness after your mom and Blaire arrived." He removed his cell phone from his back pocket. "Sawyer just texted me a schedule for their regular patrols of the property. We've got you covered."

"That means a lot to me, especially with Mom and Blaire here too." She organized the copies of her father's journal and tucked them into the folder. "I made extras just in case."

"Don't blame you. Perhaps lock the drive in the desk drawer. Keys are in the pencil holder."

She did as he suggested. "Where are Mom and Blaire?"

"I set up a table in Blaire's room so she can work in there. Your mom is—"

"Right here." Rebecca Tremblay rubbed her eyes and stepped into the office. "I had a little snooze, then heard voices and wanted to see what you're doing."

"Sorry, did we wake you?"

"It's okay, Izzy. I didn't want to sleep long anyway." She pointed to the board. "What's all this?"

Izzy grimaced. She didn't want her mother to see all of her dad's journal pages. "My evidence board for the case Dad was working on."

Her mother's eyes flashed. "Why are you still investigating? Your father died from a heart attack."

"Mom, how can you say that after everything that's happened?"

"Coincidence."

"I don't believe in those. Dad was in perfect health. He showed me his test results and I remember everything vividly." She took a breath. "And someone stuck you and Blaire in a closet, Mom. That's not a coincidence, and you know it!"

Névé lifted her head at Izzy's raised voice.

She cleared her throat. "Sorry. I'm just tired of people not trusting my intuition. And these attacks prove it's more than that. Dad was investigating something that got him killed."

Her mother's lip quivered. "I just don't want to lose anyone else."

Izzy rubbed her mother's arm. "I'm not going anywhere."

"Mrs. Tremblay, my employees are rotating their patrols of the ranch property. They'll be watching the place around the clock. The front gate is locked. No one in or out without our approval."

"I appreciate that. I realize I said earlier I didn't want your protection, but I was wrong. You're a good man, Austin."

Névé barked.

Izzy's mom giggled. "Yes, you're good too, girl." She pointed to the journal page printouts. "That's Justin's handwriting. What do these numbers mean?"

"It's a code. A message for me, but I don't know what cipher Dad used." Izzy bit her fingernails. "That's the piece of information his CI had given me before he died." She tapped her temple. "But it's within those missing three hours locked in my memory somewhere."

Her mother turned. "Well, remember what your dad always said when he couldn't figure something out?"

"'Walking is where I do my best thinking.'" Izzy lowered her voice to mimic her father's, then focused on Névé. "What do you say, girl? Wanna go for a stroll?"

The dog perked her ears up and leaped up on all fours.

Austin chuckled. "You had her at stroll. How about I take you around the property and then to my K-9 training area? I would like to show it to you."

"Sure. Mom, you wanna come?"

"No. I'm going to grab something to read from Austin's huge bookshelf and curl up by the fireplace."

"Mom, don't tell anyone about the journal, okay?"

"But why?"

How much should she tell her mother? She didn't want to

scare her, but she must protect her family. "I don't trust anyone else but us."

"Fine. I'll catch you later." She left the room.

Austin unclipped the two-way radio from his belt. "First, I
need to tell Sawyer we're going outside and to be on the lookout
for us. I don't want anything catching us off guard."

Conroy's warning that Padilla was close to figuring out Izzy's
location barreled into her head. A wave of angst slammed her
body.

Was it true and if so, how?

An arctic breeze snaked down Austin's neck, and he tightened
his blue-and-green-plaid scarf. He led a bundled Izzy around
the property to help give her both exercise and some thinking
time. Névé bounded ahead of them, playing in the snow. With
all of his men on guard, Austin felt it safe to release Névé from
her duties so she could enjoy their time together.

Izzy giggled, then hurried ahead and plopped herself beside the dog.

*Lord, I would love this to be the norm. Me and Izzy walking
on the ranch with Névé.*

The idea warmed his chilled body, but then the hurt after the
night of Clara's death slammed into his chest, stealing his breath
and icing his veins.

Izzy's silence after the call had nearly killed Austin. He had
planned to tell her his true feelings for her after their shift, but
his hesitation cost more than her friend's life. It cost him Izzy's
respect.

It took him months to move on from the woman in front of
him. Right now his ranch kept him busy, and he didn't have time
for anyone in his life.

At least, that's how he justified his single status. Truth be told,
he longed for a wife and kids to share this special place with
him. His adoptive parents had worked hard to build the ranch,
and now Austin continued their legacy.

Sometimes Austin wondered who his biological mother and father were, but he always pushed the thoughts aside. They had abandoned him as a baby, and that was hard to come back from.

Austin had vowed that if he ever had children, he would hold them close. Love them with his entire being and never let them feel unwanted.

Like his biological parents had made him feel.

Tom and Mandy Murray took him in after he'd been in and out of foster homes, loved him, and adopted him when Austin was ten years old. He was the child they could never have. "A gift from God," they often said.

The couple raised him to respect people and treat everyone with kindness. However, when he was bullied at grade school for being adopted, Austin's insecurities over his biological parents' rejection of him had multiplied. He began acting out and was suspended at one point. When questioned about his sudden change in demeanor, Austin had shared with his parents how the kids were making fun of him for being adopted, stating he wasn't loved.

Austin never forgot his father's actions and words. He pulled him into an embrace and said, "Son, being adopted is a gift. It means God loved you enough to send you into our lives for safe-keeping. Until one day, when you grow up and have kids, you can show them how love works. It's not about the bloodline. It's about love—pure and simple."

Austin smiled as the memory of his father's words brought both happiness and sadness all rolled into one. *I miss you, Mom and Dad.*

Izzy's laughter brought him back to his ranch.

God, what's my path? Will I find someone to love?

Love was Austin's deepest desire. He wanted to show love because Tom and Mandy Murray had shown him what true love meant. Both in terms of their marriage and their affection for their son. Austin.

But for now, Austin would put his love toward his dogs. He eyed Izzy. *Maybe, just maybe.* "Iz, you want to come now and see how I train the dogs?"

"Sure." She stood from making snow angels and brushed her jeans off. "Lead the way."

Moments later they entered the Murray K-9 Ranch's kennels. The large building housed all his dogs comfortably, minus Névé, and was also where he trained during the winter months. Dogs were always Austin's passion, so when he left the police department, he threw himself into learning how to train dogs. His father helped him get the ranch set up, and it soon blossomed into the lucrative business he had today—raising dogs to get them ready for K-9 units across the country.

Izzy whistled as she gazed around the building. "You have a state-of-the-art business going on here."

"Thanks. I provide dogs to police departments across Canada. Even have had interest from some in the States." Austin opened a golden retriever's cage. "This beauty is almost ready to go to the Yukon. I've been training her to become an avalanche dog. This is Penny."

Izzy squatted in front of the retriever. "Hello, Penny. You're beautiful."

Behind them, Névé whimpered.

Izzy stood. "What's wrong with her?"

"Sometimes malamutes don't play well with other dogs, especially of the same gender. And she's jealous you're giving Penny attention. Névé can be territorial." Austin picked up a nearby shovel. "Want to see how Penny can find someone in the snow?"

"Sure. How do you train them for that?"

He snickered. "You'll see. You up for a game of hide and seek?"

She tilted her head to the right, crossing her arms. "Something tells me you're using me for bait."

"Yup. First, I need to put Névé back in the house. I don't want her interfering with Penny's training."

After taking the malamute into the house and burying Izzy safely in the snow, Austin brought the golden outside and squatted in front of her. "Penny, search!"

The dog bounced through the snow, zigzagging across the yard. She stopped in various spots, sniffing the snow, then veered to a new area and back again. Seconds later she bolted directly toward where Austin had buried Izzy and dug ferociously as her tail wagged in a helicopter spiral. She'd found the avalanche victim.

Penny buried her head into the hole she dug and tugged on the rope training tool Austin had given Izzy. Moments later Izzy's snow-covered head appeared.

Austin approached the fort-like pile of snow he had constructed to train. "Good girl, Penny." He helped Izzy to her feet. "And that's how it's done."

"Impressive." Izzy rubbed Penny's head. "She's so smart. When is she going to the Yukon?"

Too soon for Austin's liking. "In a couple of weeks, her handler will return to complete her final training. He's been coming every month for a week at a time. They've bonded well. I insist on that before I let my dogs go. It's part of the contract."

"It must be hard to give up the dogs after training them."

Was Izzy reading his mind again? "It is, but I want all different agencies to benefit from what these animals can do. They simply amaze me more and more every day."

Snowflakes floated in front of them before multiplying. The wind picked up and rattled his flagpole nearby.

"You ready to head in? Looks like the storm is intensifying." Austin swept snow off the golden.

"Yes. Being buried chilled me to the bone. Think I'll join Mom in front of that fire." She rubbed her gloved hands together.

"Let me get Penny back into her home and I'll—"

A gunshot echoed throughout the property, sending more than weather chills down Austin's back.

Had Padilla breached the Murray K-9 Ranch?

NINE

Izzy dropped into the snow and yanked Penny down with her, protecting the dog from harm. "Austin, where did the shot come from?" Had Padilla and his men found them? Rapid-fire heartbeats constricted her chest, sending her pulse throbbing in her head.

"Sawyer! Who's shooting?" Austin yelled into his radio.

Multiple dogs barked from the kennels, and Penny squirmed beneath Izzy's hold. "It's okay, girl. I've got you."

When no response came, Austin pressed the button again. "Sawyer, report!"

Shouts filled the air moments before Sawyer and a few ranch hands raced around the corner of the K-9 building, each carrying rifles.

Izzy pushed herself into a crouched position, staying low in case of more gunfire.

Sawyer approached. "Movement spotted at the property edge. Izzy, I suggest you get inside. We're going to inspect the grounds."

Austin clipped his radio back on his belt. "Who fired?"

A blond man in his late twenties raised his hand. "I did, Austin. I was the one who spotted someone suspicious on the south side."

Austin frowned. "Well, did they fire first, Maverick? I only heard the one shot."

Maverick—the new guy.

Izzy read Austin's wrenched face. He was upset. Why the harsh tone? Had Maverick given them issues since his arrival?

The man switched his hold on the rifle to his left hand. "I saw a gun."

"Are you sure? You're too trigger happy." Austin took the rifle from him. "Please go clean out the north stable."

Maverick's expression morphed into something else before it vanished and he stomped away, but Izzy caught it.

Deceit? Contempt?

Did Austin see it too?

Maverick's attitude didn't sit well with Izzy. Her police intuition's warning bells screamed deceit.

Sawyer shifted his stance. "Don't be so hard on him, Austin. He's—"

"New." Austin threw his hands in the air. "You keep defending him, Sawyer. Why?"

The ranch foreman's gaze lowered to the ground. "Something about him reminds me of myself at his age."

"You vetted him, so I'm trusting our lives with your instincts." Austin addressed the other men. "Do another perimeter sweep. Find whoever was lurking. I need to ensure Izzy and her family are safe."

Izzy withdrew her cell phone. "I'll get Doug to have an officer patrol the area." She reached her partner and explained the situation. He agreed to have someone drive around Austin's ranch. Izzy clicked off the call.

Sawyer barked orders at the men, and they scattered in different directions.

"Iz, let's get Penny in her kennel and you back inside." Austin placed his hand on her lower back and nudged her toward the K-9 building.

"How long has Maverick been working here?" Izzy reached the door first, opening it for him and Penny.

"A month now." Austin ran his hands over the golden's body before opening her kennel. "You're good, Penny." He tossed her a treat. "Your reward for finding Iz in the snow."

Penny woofed before catching the bone-shaped snack.

Izzy chuckled at their interaction. She was impressed at how well Austin was doing with his K-9 training. Her father would say God turned ashes into beauty as He knew Austin's path would lead him here—where he was meant to be.

Was that true? Did God know what lay beyond the path's bend?

Because right now, Izzy couldn't see through the fog.

Austin poured water into Penny's dish and closed the kennel door. "I didn't mean to be so abrupt with Maverick. He's just been making too many mistakes and he could have gotten himself—or you—killed by his recklessness."

"Can I be honest?"

"Of course." Austin opened the door for her.

"I get the sense something is off about Maverick. You know, that cop intuition thing." Izzy strode outside.

The snowflakes now blanketed the property with a white wall. Izzy readjusted her scarf and followed Austin back to the ranch house. The fire was calling her name, and she couldn't wait to send its warmth into her chilled body.

Once inside, Austin stomped the snow from his boots and took off his coat. "I agree, Iz. I can't put my finger on it, but lately Maverick has been—what's the word I'm looking for—almost sneaky. Sawyer assures me he came with positive recommendations from the last ranch where he worked."

"Why did he leave there?" Izzy wiggled out of her coat and hung it on the wall hook.

Névé bounded into the hallway and snuggled into her.

Austin chuckled. "She doesn't always warm up to people so quickly."

Or maybe she sensed Izzy's emerging feelings toward her handler. Izzy squatted in front of the dog and kissed her forehead, suppressing her emotion. "Shall we go get warmed up, girl?"

Névé barked.

Izzy moved into the living room and noted an opened book

turned upside down on the rocker. However, her mother was no-where in sight. Once her mother got her nose in a novel, nothing could distract her. Perhaps she went to the kitchen for a snack.

Izzy walked to the fireplace and held her hands out in front of the flames. "You didn't answer my question."

"Maverick claims he wants experience training dogs and found out about my ranch through my website." Austin removed the poker from its hook, jabbed the coals, then threw another log on the fire. "But I'm not ready to train him. Is that mean of me?" He positioned himself beside her, holding out his hands.

His powerful presence gave her a sense of protection, re-newed friendship, and—

Dare she hope for more?

"There's nothing wrong with being cautious, Austin. I realize you still have that cop intuition, so trust your gut." Izzy swept a stray curl off his forehead.

Their eyes locked, holding in place.

Austin looked away, breaking the connection. "I need to check with Sawyer on the perimeter. Névé, stay." He unclipped his radio and spoke into it as he exited the room.

Izzy's shoulders slumped. *Remember, he never felt the same as you. Don't forget about Dax.*

Between the two heartaches, she couldn't—and wouldn't—love again.

The pain went too deep.

And that's something she'll never forget.

Névé trotted over to her and licked her hand.

At least someone loved her.

Thumping footfalls tensed her already tightened muscles.

Austin reappeared. "Your uncle is at the front gate, demand-ing to talk to you. Says he may be able to help you with your father's coded journal pages."

Izzy's jaw dropped. "But how did Uncle Ford find out about those?"

"I told him." Her mother entered the room, carrying a glass of water.

Why couldn't her mother trust Izzy's instincts and leave things alone? "Mom, I told you not to tell anyone."

"Your uncle is not just anyone. He's family and feels he can help." She picked up her book from the rocking chair and sat. "Blaire is finishing up work and coming too."

Izzy cemented her hands at her side.

Austin held up his cell phone. "Iz, do I let him in?"

She nodded.

Perhaps her mother was right. After all, Uncle Ford knew his brother well.

And right now, she'd welcome any help in solving this case.

Before more people were targeted.

Austin placed a tray of warm muffins in the middle of his dining room table. Izzy had pulled him aside and suggested they meet here instead of his office. She didn't want to compromise the case by having anyone else seeing the evidence board. The pictures and her notes were police business. He agreed and helped her spread the copies of her father's journal pages in the middle of the table. Austin made a fresh pot of coffee and poured everyone a cup.

Sawyer had informed Austin that his men secured the property. No sign of the person Maverick had supposedly seen. Sawyer reported fresh footprints near the fence, confirming Maverick's claim. Izzy had shared that the officer cruising the area had seen nothing suspicious.

But that didn't mean someone wasn't out there.

Izzy put a muffin on her plate. "Uncle Ford, what makes you think you can crack this code?"

The man fingered his mustache. "Because I knew Justin longer than any of you. We weren't born twins, but sure had the same tendencies. I understand how he used to think."

Blaire broke a muffin in two. "And remember, Uncle Ford almost became a cop, too. He has the street smarts."

Austin didn't miss the praise in Blaire's tone.

Or Izzy's contorted expression.

Why such a drastic difference between sisters? What had warranted the friction between the two?

And why had Izzy distanced herself from her uncle? Austin had seen it the moment he entered the ranch. Ford had hugged her, but Izzy's rigid body screamed with annoyance.

Was it because of his attention to her mother?

Ford patted Blaire's hand. "You're too kind."

Izzy coughed, then stuffed a bite of her muffin into her mouth.

Austin had been away from his ex-partner for years, but still could read her expressions. He placed his hand on hers and mouthed, *You okay?*

She dipped her chin in response before turning to the group. "Let's begin. What I know is, Dad used a code and right before his CI was killed, Sims shared the cipher with me." She tapped her temple. "But it's locked in that three-hour window I can't remember."

"Odd that Miss Perfect Memory can't remember something," Blaire huffed, then sipped her coffee.

Austin read the jealousy on Blaire's face and the pain on Izzy's. Clearly, the Tremblay sisters were at odds.

He remembered Izzy telling him they were close. Inseparable was the word she used.

He caught Izzy's expression before she pointed to the print-outs on the table. "You'll see that Dad used a series of numbers. Everyone grab a printout and see if anything jumps out at you."

The group did as Izzy instructed. Silence filled the room as each observed the numbers.

"I've looked into different ciphers, but honestly, I don't know which one Dad would have used." Izzy slammed the paper she held on to the table and stood.

Névé jumped up from her position in the corner, alert to Izzy's sudden moves.

"I think we need to pray about this." Ford returned the printout he'd been holding to the table and reached for Rebecca and Blaire's hands.

Izzy whirled around, her eyes flashing venom.

Not good. Austin needed to intervene before the situation got messy. He raised his hand to stop any words he guessed she was about to say. "I think prayer is a good idea." He patted Izzy's seat. "Come sit, Iz."

She exhaled. "Fine, but can you pray, Austin?"

"Sure." Austin stole a peek at Ford.

The man's countenance transformed from lovable into an unreadable emotion. Frustration? Anger?

Ignoring the question of why the animosity between uncle and niece existed, Austin bowed his head. "Father, we come to You today requesting Your help. Izzy needs to remember what Sims told her regarding her father's cipher. Please give us all direction in helping solve the mystery. We also pray for protection from whoever is trying to do this family harm." Should he also pray for family unity? *Son, always listen to God's still, small voice.* Something his father said and right now, that voice nudged Austin. "Also, can you bring this family closer? They need each other during these rough patches. We pray this in Your precious name. Amen."

He stole a glimpse at Ford.

The man stared at Izzy's bowed head. Even though his earlier expression had been unreadable, the one on his face now revealed an emotion that spiked Austin's guard.

Contempt.

Why did the man hold anger toward his niece?

Blaire snagged her cell phone. "I'm going to search on ciphers. I realize you did, Izzy, but maybe talking about them among us will spark something."

"Great idea, Blaire." Ford snatched a muffin and took a bite.

"Okay, here's what comes up for ciphers. Transposition, concealment." Blaire continued to read from the list of common ciphers.

Rebecca slammed her hand on the table. "Wait, isn't there one about using books? At least, I've seen that in the movies. Justin loved to read." She turned to Izzy. "Remember how he used to read to you?"

"Yeah, his favorite." Blaire tossed her phone back onto the table.

"Not true, Blaire. He just knew you didn't like to read. When he tried, you always hid under the covers and hummed to yourself. I'm hardly his—" Izzy shot to her feet, then paced around the table.

"What is it, Iz?" Austin stood and placed his hand on her shoulder, stopping her meandering.

"I think Sims may have told me that Dad used the book cipher and that I just have to figure out the reference book."

Blaire leaned back in her chair, crossing her arms. "Hmm. Well, that's like finding a needle in a haystack. You have a ton of books, sister. Use that memory of yours to figure it out."

"I wish it was that easy." Izzy plunked onto her chair and held her head in her hands.

"What do you mean?" Rebecca shifted a paper toward her. "How does it work? What do the numbers signify?"

Austin ignored Blaire's poor attitude and pointed to the printout. "Each number refers to a page, line and word on that line. However, the key is to use the correct book and edition or the code is useless."

Izzy hissed out a breath. "I have no idea what book he would have used. I can picture each on my bookshelf, but none that stand out."

Ford's phone dinged and he swiped the screen. "I gotta get to a special police board meeting."

Izzy tilted her head. "I thought they were the last Wednesday of each month."

"They are, but the mayor called this one. Something about urgent business." Ford placed his hand on Rebecca's arm. "Call if you need anything."

She nodded.

Ford gestured toward the printouts. "I hope you understand my brother's cryptic notes, Izzy. Catch you all later."

"I'll walk you out." Austin led him out of the dining room and into the hallway. He lifted Ford's coat from the hook and handed it to him. "Have a good evening."

Ford poked Austin's chest. "You stay out of Izzy's life. You almost ruined her ten years ago. Don't do it again."

Wait—what? Heat singed Austin's face, and he fought to suppress his anger. "I'm only offering a place of refuge for her and her family. That's all." *Liar.* Austin hated that the man had obviously read the emotions Austin battled to keep under wraps.

"I don't like that you've conveniently come back into her life. I don't trust you, dog man." He stomped out of the house, leaving a menacing tone lingering in the air.

And Austin wondering who they could trust.

TEN

Izzy stepped outside later that evening with Névé on one side and Austin on the other. Lingering snowflakes floated to the ground, and Izzy tipped her face toward the sky. She opened her mouth and let the frozen white droplets fall on her tongue. Something she and Blaire used to do as kids. The thought of Izzy's strained relationship with her sister made her clamp her mouth shut, blocking out the memories. After supper, Izzy had invited her family to go on a walk around the property. Sawyer claimed the ranch was secure, and no one lurked in the shadows. However, both Blaire and their mother said they were retiring after a long, stressful day. Seemed all the talk about ciphers and her father's case had tuckered her family out.

Probably for the best. Izzy had had enough of her family for one day. Austin had mentioned Uncle Ford's hostility toward him as he left. Right now, she only wanted a peaceful evening. After all, what more could she ask for—a handsome man, a sweet dog and stillness in the fresh air? Izzy breathed in.

I could get used to this.

"What are you thinking?" Austin's baritone voice added to her romantic dreams.

If only you could read my mind. Then again, that probably wouldn't be a good thing. "Just how peaceful it is here." Best leave it at that. Anything more may expose the feelings she struggled to contain. She had to slam the box shut and throw away the key if her heart was going to survive being so close to Austin Murray. "You sure it's safe for a walk?"

"The ranch hand on duty just reported everything was quiet,

so we're good." Austin scooped up some snow and chucked it. "Névé, catch."

The dog barked and bounded across the field, jumping to catch the snowball.

"I'm sorry about Uncle Ford's harsh treatment. He had no right to do that."

"What's his story, anyway? I never met him when we were partners, and you didn't talk about him much. Was your dad younger or older than Ford?"

"Older. Uncle Ford grew up in the shadow of my father and always wanted to be like Justin Tremblay. He followed him into the police academy but didn't make it. Uncle Ford was devastated but happy with how well Dad did." Izzy kicked at a mound of snow. "He went on to further his career in science and works for a pharmaceutical company. He's done really well for himself."

"I get the impression he favors Blaire over you, or is that just my imagination?" Austin pointed left. "Let's go this way."

Izzy turned in the direction he suggested and rounded the corner of the ranch. The horse stable was well lit with a powerful floodlight over the top of the large red barn doors. "It's not your imagination. Blaire has always been Uncle Ford's favorite. Not exactly sure why. Maybe because she's the younger sibling, like him."

"Can I ask you a question?"

Izzy hesitated. How personal did she want to get with this man? Could she go there again? Their friendship had been deep, and she missed their talks. She breathed in and took the plunge. "Sure."

"What happened between you and Blaire? You used to be so close when we were partners."

Not the question she was expecting. She'd figured he'd ask about her love life as he used to tease her relentlessly about the lack of men in her life. How much could she reveal when she didn't really understand Blaire's secrecy herself? She let out an audible breath.

"That bad? Sorry if I'm interfering where I shouldn't. I realize we haven't seen each other in a while."

"To be honest I'm not sure myself. A couple of years ago, I discovered something questionable about the man she was dating." Izzy pictured the case that had come across her desk vividly. "I was working on a missing children's case, and when the father's picture came on my screen, I was shocked. It was Blaire's boyfriend, Luca. He was married with two children and a suspect in his daughter's disappearance." Once again, Izzy lifted her face toward the sky and let the snowflakes fall like feathers onto her skin. Something about the snow felt like cleansing to Izzy. Winter was her favorite season. "We questioned Luca, but he had a solid alibi."

They walked to the edge of the ranch property, near the tree line. Thankfully, the fence kept intruders from breaching the premises—at least that's what Sawyer claimed.

Austin whistled. "Wow. How did Blaire take it?"

"Not good. She wouldn't believe me, so I invited both Blaire and Luca over to my condo, then confronted him." She'd never forget Luca's anger or the hurt in Blaire's saddened eyes. However, her hurt was directed more toward Izzy than her married boyfriend. "He told Blaire he and his wife were in the middle of a messy divorce. I didn't believe him. Blaire did."

"You mean she kept seeing him?"

"Yup. Even after Mom and Dad's insistence that she break up with him." Izzy puffed out a breath and watched it linger in the frosty night air. "They finally broke up a year ago, but she wouldn't tell me why. Ever since I told her Luca was married, our relationship changed and Uncle Ford took her side in everything. Yelled at me for interfering."

"I'm sorry. You were only trying to help. She should have known you were doing it out of love."

A coyote howled, interrupting the serenity on the ranch property.

Névé growled, positioning herself in front of Izzy and Austin.

Seconds later another coyote answered from the opposite direction—and louder. The animal was close.

Were they marking their territory?

A shudder prickled Izzy's spine, and she clutched Austin's arm. "That was too close. Do coyotes often come on your property?"

"Sometimes. Normally, the barking dogs keep them away." Austin guided her toward the ranch house. "Let's head back."

"Good idea. I've had enough excitement for one day. I don't want to add a coyote confrontation to the list."

"Névé, come," Austin commanded.

The malamute obeyed, trotting beside Izzy.

"She's well-trained." Izzy was impressed with Austin's skills. "You've done well for yourself here."

"Thanks. Training dogs is my passion and even though the path to get here was rough, I feel it's what God called me to do."

She knew Austin spoke about the night Clara was killed. Was he finally ready to talk about it? "Austin, what—" Her cell phone buzzed, interrupting her question. She fished it out from her coat pocket and checked the screen. Doug. She hit the answer button. "Hey, partner, what's up?"

"Sorry, I realize it's late, but I had to give you a quick call. Two things. We've connected the King & Sons shell corp to a known drug ring funding the community with those bath salts. Plus the coroner has linked a recent drug overdose death to the same drug, but says whoever is making the salts has modified them to be more deadly."

Izzy stopped in front of the ranch house steps. "No! We need to stop Padilla. That was the drug Dad was investigating."

"Anything more on the journal?"

"Getting closer, but no. What's the second thing you called for?"

Névé bounded up the stairs, with Austin close behind.

"A warning. The chief constable will call you. Something about a board meeting."

Did it have to do with the impromptu meeting her uncle had dashed off to? "Great. That's all I need." Her phone buzzed. She checked the screen. "That's him now. Thanks for the update." She followed Austin and his dog into the ranch foyer.

"Stay safe."

"You too." Izzy clicked off Doug's call and turned to Austin. "Halt is calling. I gotta take this."

He nodded. "I'll get us some lavender tea."

Izzy smiled. He always knew what made her relax. That was her favorite tea to settle her nerves.

She stomped the snow from her boots and kicked them off before moving into the living room, hitting the speaker icon. "Tremblay here."

"Sorry for calling so late, Isabelle."

Isabelle? First Izzy and now Isabelle. Something was definitely wrong. "No worries. What's going on?"

A sigh sailed through the speaker. "I told you to stay at the ranch, but the police board has called an important meeting tomorrow that you need to go to."

"Did something happen at the meeting tonight?"

"How did you find out? It was called at the last minute."

Izzy placed the phone on the coffee table and wiggled out of her coat. "Uncle Ford was here and left quickly to attend. He's on the executive board. Why do I have to go?"

"The mayor received an anonymous tip about you, and now I'm under review for allowing you to help with Ned Bolton's interview. I tried to explain the situation, but Georgia—Mayor Fox—wouldn't listen. She's convinced you acted inappropriately. I disagree with her claims, but you need to come in and defend yourself."

Izzy plunked herself into a plush plaid chair. "And you."

Névé whined and nestled her snout on Izzy's lap.

The dog had obviously sensed Izzy's shift in emotions.

She stroked Névé's head. "Did she give you details?"

"She said she'd present everything at the meeting."

"When and where is it, sir?"

"Harturn River Library at eight thirty tomorrow morning."

Austin appeared holding two mugs, but hesitated at the entranceway.

She waved him in. She needed his support right now. "Okay, sir. I'll be there."

"Isabelle, please be careful. Can you get Austin and his dog to protect you? You know how short-staffed we are here. We assigned all the constables to cases at the moment."

Izzy's gaze shifted to Austin. She raised a brow in a silent question.

He dipped his head, confirming his help.

"He's in, but what are you thinking?"

"I don't like the timing of these allegations. Something is off to me, and it might only be a ploy to get you to come out of hiding."

Izzy leaned forward, disturbing Névé.

Could her chief be right and she was walking into a trap?

Austin tossed and turned on his king-size bed as nightmares held him in their haunting grip, plunging him back to a seven-year-old cowering behind a hay bale. He shivered—not from the cold—but from the wrath of the man who threatened to whip him. Again. All because Austin had eaten the last cookie.

"You can't hide, Austin." His foster father's voice boomed in the large barn. "You have to pay for disobeying me."

Why did you leave me, Mom and Dad? The recurring question had followed him to every foster care home he'd been sent to. Tears flowed down his cheeks as he hugged his knees to his chest, attempting to make himself as small as possible.

Maybe then *he* wouldn't find him.

Austin's battered body couldn't take much more of the man's fury.

Scratching sounded nearby. What was his foster father doing?

Whoosh!

A glow appeared over the hay bale. Seconds later smoke filled the barn and Austin sneezed, giving away his location.

The man sneered as he towered over Austin, holding his whip. "There you are."

More scratching followed by dogs barking.

Austin raised his hands. "Please don't hurt me. I'm sorry I ate the last cookie. I was so hungry. I'll never do it again. I promise."

"It's too late for your sorry excuses." The man cracked the whip. "Time for your punishment."

The scene morphed and a different man stood behind a whimpering woman, holding a gun to her temple. "Stay back or my wife dies."

The woman's bruised and battered face confirmed the man's capabilities. Clearly, if he'd done that to her already, he'd follow through on his threat to kill his wife.

Austin tensed as something in the man's expression reminded him of his foster father from when he was seven. The multiple blows he'd inflicted returned tenfold, sending Austin into a stupor. His mind and body suspended in time, eliminating any takedown scenarios from emerging.

Clara and Izzy yelled, but their cries were muffled in his trancelike state.

A shot rang out and Clara dropped, blood appearing on her chest.

"No!" Austin jerked upright in his bed, jolting himself awake. His pulse pounded in his head. Two horrifying scenes from his past thrust together into one jumbled nightmare. Again? What had prompted the dream to return after years of silence?

Névé barked and scratched at Austin's door, dragging him back to reality.

Smoke seeped through the opened window. Even in the dead of winter, Austin left it cracked open for ventilation. Where was it coming from? It had also invaded his dream.

A glow flickered behind the slats in his blinds. *What is that?*

Austin thrust his comforter aside, vaulting out of bed. He flew to the window and raised the blinds. The sight before him seized his breath and locked his muscles.

Flames crawled up the sides of his K-9 training building like a monster reaching for its innocent victim. "No!"

His dogs were in danger, and he had to save them.

ELEVEN

Austin nabbed his cell phone and radio before yanking open the door, nearly colliding with his malamute. "Névé, come!" Austin had started training the dog in search and rescue when she was about twelve weeks old, but how would she handle a fire? Austin raced through the house, yelling, "Fire!" He reached Izzy's room and pounded on her door. "Izzy, get up! Fire!"

Névé barked.

The door swung open and a wide-eyed Izzy appeared. "What's going on?"

"K-9 building's on fire. Get your mom and sister out of the house in case it spreads. Now!" He didn't wait for an answer but veered into the hall and pressed an alarm button he had installed for occasions such as this. It would alert everyone on the premises.

The siren pierced through the ranch house and across the property.

Pounding footfalls above him revealed Sawyer was leaving his room in the loft.

Austin didn't wait, but snatched his coat from the hook and fled into the night as he hit 911 on his phone, requesting emergency services. After disconnecting, Austin called the on-call vet for his region. He hated to phone so late, but guessed his dogs would need Dr. Sarah Gardner's services. She agreed to come to his ranch immediately. *Lord, please save the dogs.*

Despite the growing heat from the fire, the freezing winter air stung his exposed skin, and Austin put on his coat and gloves quickly.

Sawyer bounded down the steps. "The guys are getting every hose and bucket that will reach the building."

They could barely hear muffled barks above Austin's siren. "Good. You've confirmed they're out of their cabins?"

"Yes."

Austin hit a button before pocketing his phone. The alert silenced, and the barking grew louder. "Let's go. We need to get to the dogs."

"We're coming too!" Izzy yelled from the doorway. Rebecca and Blaire followed her down the steps.

Austin pointed to the stable. "Sawyer, get the horses out. Just in case. Send someone to guard the north stable and the cattle. I'll work with the others on the flames."

Sawyer nodded and ran to the large red stable doors, yelling for another ranch hand to help.

Austin beelined toward the K-9 building, the women close behind. Maverick had hooked up the long hose and sprayed the door. How had he gotten there so quickly? Austin ignored his question, thankful for his help, and instructed the others to form a line to the faucet on the side of the stable. They obeyed and quickly filled bucket after bucket, dousing the flames enough to clear a path to the entrance.

Austin pointed to the group. "Izzy, I'm going in. I need to get the dogs out. You help with the bucket brigade. We need to get the flames out as much as we can. Firefighters are about ten minutes away."

She latched on to his coat sleeve. "It's too dangerous. You can't go in."

"I have to." Austin placed a mask over his mouth and wrenched the door open.

Heat assaulted him as if he'd stepped into a large oven. He stumbled backward. The flames had reached inside the building.

Dogs barked. Some whimpered.

Lord, please help me. I need to save them.

Névé bolted around Austin's legs and darted through the entranceway.

"No! Retreat, Névé!"

She continued inside. The malamute rarely ignored Austin's commands, but this time she was on a mission.

Save her friends.

Austin inched through the doors and made his way to each of the dog's cages. He unlocked them and opened each one. "Cover!" he commanded, pointing toward the entrance.

Penny, Thor, Hunter and five others fled their smoky prisons into the night.

Névé whimpered.

Austin turned at his dog's cry.

And gasped.

Névé tugged an unconscious Goose by the collar, dragging the shepherd around the wall of flames, intent on one thing.

Getting Goose to safety.

Thankfully, his malamute had the strength to haul heavy objects.

One dog left.

Austin hustled to the end of the row and unlocked Wolf's door. The Belgian Malinois lay silent on the floor. "No!" Austin scooped the dog into his arms and staggered through the building.

Flames erupted in front of Austin, blocking his path. *No! Lord, help.*

A blurred image of Maverick appeared in the doorway overtop of the blaze. "I've got you!" He aimed the hose at the flames and sprayed.

They sizzled and additional smoke rose higher.

Austin coughed through his mask while he waited for Maverick to unblock the path to the door.

Finally, after what seemed like an eternity, the flames dissipated. The sixty-five-pound dog slowed him down, but Austin ignored the weight depleting the strength in his arms and continued toward the entrance.

Sirens pierced the night as the flashing lights from the fire trucks, police cruiser and an ambulance lit up the ranch property.

Seconds later the vet's vehicle sped down the driveway.

Help had arrived.

Relief relaxed Austin's grip, and he dropped to his knees to set Wolf on the ground. He whipped off his mask and gulped in the cold winter air. "Come on, boy. Come back to me." He checked for a pulse and found a steady one. *Thank you.*

Izzy raced to his side. "Is he okay?"

"Not sure. The vet just arrived. Can you get her here right away?"

She nodded and dashed back toward the ranch house.

Austin searched for his dogs while rubbing Wolf's body. He found them in the distance with Névé barking commands. She had rounded them up like a perfect search and rescue dog.

Good girl.

Also, Goose had regained consciousness. *Thank You, Lord.* Austin turned back to Wolf. He was the only one still in jeopardy.

Firefighters had joined Austin's crew and soon had their hoses aimed on the K-9 building. Thankfully, they had prevented the flames from spreading to the stables, cabins and his ranch house. Constable Fisher spoke to the fire chief.

Rushed movements caught his attention. Dr. Sarah Gardner stumbled through the snow with Izzy by her side. The vet's mobile backpack jostled as she ran.

Austin waved. "Over here!"

Sarah reached Wolf and dropped to the ground. "Hey, Austin. How is he?" She wiggled out of the backpack's hold and unzipped the bag, withdrawing a stethoscope.

Izzy waited nearby.

"Still unconscious, but breathing." Austin's fingers grazed Sarah's arm. "Please save him."

"You know I'll do my best." She glanced back at the other dogs. "I see Névé is keeping her friends away from the blaze."

"She actually hauled an unconscious Goose from the building." Austin bit the inside of his mouth. "They will all need to be checked out."

A horse whinnied nearby.

"And the horses," Sarah added.

"Sawyer got them out and the flames never reached the stable, but to be on the safe side, yes, they should be. Do you need to call in help?"

"Figured I'd need it after you explained the situation, so I already did. The vet from a couple of towns over is on his way." She listened to Wolf's heart. "It's strong. He'll be—"

"Austin!" Sawyer hurried toward them. "You need to see this." He held his tablet in the air.

Austin flew to his feet. "What is it?"

"One ranch hand took this on the east side of the property." Sawyer clicked the screen and handed the tablet to Austin.

A photo of a hole cut in his electrified barbed wire fence.

Austin froze.

Someone had breached the premises, leading Austin to one conclusion.

The fire wasn't an accident.

Izzy noted the alarm on Austin's face after looking at Sawyer's tablet. She darted to his side. "What is it?"

Austin turned the tablet in her direction. "Someone cut the fence. Sawyer, how did they do it without being electrocuted?"

Izzy's hand flew to cover her mouth, but not in time to stifle her quick intake of breath.

The two men peered at her.

"What are you thinking, Iz?" Austin handed the tablet back to Sawyer.

Dare she give them her thoughts? She caught Austin's gaze. "You won't like it."

"You feel it was an inside job?" Austin fisted his hands.

"Someone had to have turned off the power to the fence, so the suspect could cut the barbed wire." Izzy waved at Fisher, gesturing him to come over. "We need to get forensics here."

Fisher raised his index finger, indicating he'd be there momentarily.

Sawyer crossed his arms, hugging his tablet. "But if it was an inside job, why wouldn't the person just open the front gate? It would have been easier."

Austin let out a heavy sigh. "Because there's no camera on that side of the property. Remember, I spoke about adding one as it's a blind spot." He pounded on his leg. "I should have done that."

"But we've vetted all our ranch hands, Austin." Sawyer shook his head. "No, I don't think one of them did it. You know we can turn the fence on and off remotely with our new technology. Why couldn't someone else hack into our system and do the same thing?"

Austin stared at Maverick as the ranch hand watched the firefighters.

Did Austin suspect the newest member of his crew?

"Sawyer's right. Someone could have done that. I'm probably wrong." Izzy read the frustration on his face. She understood how he thought. He blamed himself for this attack.

Fisher approached. "What's going on?"

Izzy pointed to the tablet. "Sawyer, show him the picture."

The ranch foreman held it up and Fisher viewed the screen, then whistled. "Someone got through your fence." He turned to Izzy. "You think whoever did that started the fire?"

"I do, but we don't know for sure the fire was arson." Izzy noticed her mother and sister petting the dogs. Anger burned inside Izzy, and she bit the inside of her mouth to stop it from rising. However, the thought of someone purposely setting fire to the K-9 building tore at her heart.

"I'm going to check on the horses." Sawyer hurried toward

the side paddock containing the animals. Thankfully a ranch hand reported that the cattle and other animals were safe in the stable at the side of the property.

"Austin, Wolf is awake and Randall is here to help," Sarah yelled from her position, pointing to a lone male figure approaching across the yard.

"Thank You, God. I need to get all the dogs into the stable." Austin left the group to meet the second vet.

Emotions attacked Izzy as she watched Austin speak with Randall before pointing to Névé and the other dogs. She could tell by his angered expression that Austin was concerned about his animals. Izzy turned back to Fisher. "We need to treat this as arson, as that's what my gut is telling me."

"And a Tremblay gut is always right, is that it?"

She didn't miss his sarcasm. "Fisher, let's work together on this, okay? We're a team."

He scowled. "Well, you certainly don't act that way with all of your secret investigations."

Excited voices rose from the charred K-9 building, interrupting their conversation. Izzy pivoted to study the scene.

The lights from the property revealed a firefighter raising what appeared to be a jerrican.

"Looks like your suspicions are correct, Tremblay. Since you're officially on vacation, I'll handle this." Fisher trudged in the snow over to the firefighters.

Austin approached, with Névé by his side. "What's going on?"

She gestured toward Fisher and the firefighter. "My guess is they found the cause of the fire and it wasn't an accident." Izzy cupped his gloved hand with hers. "I'm so sorry. I feel like this is all my fault."

"It's not yours, it's mine. I've been procrastinating on getting a camera on that area of the ranch."

"Stop. You always blame yourself when you shouldn't." Izzy released his hand and bent to pet Névé. "You're a brave girl."

"She is. Névé saved not only Goose but all the dogs. She alerted me by scratching on my door." He rubbed the malamute's head.

"Can I look at your security system? You know I'm good with computers, plus we can check your video footage."

"Tremblay, I need to talk to you and Austin." Fisher approached with the chief in tow.

Austin leaned closer. "That doesn't sound good."

"Nope." Izzy waited for the duo to reach them. "What's going on?"

Fisher gestured toward the chief. "You know Chief Hammond, right?"

"Yes," Izzy and Austin said simultaneously.

"Tell them what you told me, Chief."

"Blaze is out now. Thanks for your good work in slowing it down." Chief Hammond slapped Austin on the back.

"Thank you and your firefighters, Chief. Is it safe to move the horses and dogs into the stable?"

"Yes, the stable is far enough away, but we'll continue to monitor everything for a bit."

Austin removed his two-way radio from his coat pocket. "Sawyer, move the animals into the stable. Dogs too. We'll have to figure out later where we'll house them. I just want them out of the cold now."

"On it, bro." Sawyer's voice crackled through the speaker.

"Bad news though. Definitely arson." Chief Hammond paused. "We found the jerrican, but it appears the fire's only point of origin was the entrance."

"So what does that mean, Chief?" Austin once again pocketed his radio.

"Not entirely sure, but I'm guessing whoever set the fire didn't want to do lots of damage."

"Tremblay, I believe the fire was some type of distraction." Fisher shifted his stance. "The question is why?"

Izzy's jaw dropped. "To get us out of the ranch house."

Fisher tilted his head. "Why?"

Izzy addressed Austin, ignoring Fisher's question. "We need to get back inside. Now!" She stumbled through the deep snow with one thing on her mind.

The flash drive and prints containing her father's notes.

Behind her, Fisher yelled at her to wait up, but she didn't have time to respond. She looked over her shoulder, noting both Névé and Austin had followed. Izzy reached the ranch house and bounded up the steps, stopping only to remove her boots. She sprinted into Austin's office and searched the desk where she'd left the flash drive.

Gone.

She eyed the evidence board.

Printouts of her father's journal.

Gone.

"No!" She fled the room and almost collided with Austin. "Stolen." Not that she couldn't recall the number sequences, but right now she didn't trust her supposedly perfect memory. Those missing three hours from the night of her attack still hadn't returned.

"What about your second set?"

"That's where I'm headed. Please pray." Not that it would probably help. She ran to her bedroom and checked where she hid the copies. In an envelope taped behind a wall picture.

She gently eased the picture's bottom edge away from the wall and reached under. Her fingers grazed the envelope. Relief washed over her tense body, thankful she had listened to her gut and hid the prints. "Thank you." Maybe God was listening after all.

"They there?"

Izzy turned at Austin's question. "Yes."

"Awesome. Let's put them in the safe. Sawyer and I are the only ones who know the combination."

Izzy wrenched the envelope from the hiding spot. "Good idea." She bit her lip. "I can't believe someone set your K-9 building on fire to get the thumb drive. If they could bypass your security, why not just kill us?"

Austin took off his gloves. "Because it *was* an inside job. Perhaps someone paid one of my ranch hands to get the drive, knowing they wouldn't also murder someone."

Izzy pictured his long look at Maverick earlier. "You're thinking Maverick?"

"Unfortunately, yes. He's the newest hand here on the ranch."

If Padilla could get to one of Austin's staff, that meant—

He knew where she was hiding.

TWELVE

Austin waited for Fisher and the forensic team to complete their search for evidence in his house. Anger rose, and he refrained from pounding the stable's wall. The group had gathered there while the team dusted for prints and searched for signs of the perp. Had it been Maverick who'd helped Padilla breach the Murray K-9 Ranch? Austin prayed that wasn't the case.

It was now three thirty in the morning, but it seemed no one would go to bed. The excitement had given them all a caffeine-like shot. However, the question remained…how long before they crashed?

Sawyer and the men constructed makeshift kennels at the back of the heated stable, so the dogs could stay there until the K-9 building was repaired. The vets had examined and treated all the dogs. The horses were unaffected by the fire. Austin praised God for saving all his animals. He didn't know what he'd do if any of them had died. He stabbed his pitchfork into the hay repeatedly.

"That hay giving you problems?" Izzy chuckled and picked up another pitchfork. "Let me help."

Austin clenched his jaw. "I'm so angry that one of my men may have helped the perp."

"We don't know that for sure. Remember, I want to check your system as soon as Fisher gives us permission to go back inside."

"Shouldn't your digital forensics do that? You don't want to get in trouble."

"Hmm. Seems I already am. I have to go in front of the police board in a few hours, remember?"

"Right." Austin jabbed another fork full and threw the hay into his favorite horse's stall. Austin had bought Jasper five years ago, and they'd been a team ever since. They enjoyed long rides across the area.

"Did you talk to your men?"

"Yes, Sawyer and I spoke to everyone. They all deny aiding the perp or starting the fire."

"And Maverick?"

Austin stopped working and leaned on the pitchfork. "I think I'm rusty after ten years of no police work. I can't get a read on him, but something bothers me. Just can't put my finger on it yet."

"Want me to do a deep dive on him? Give you peace of mind?"

Austin blew out a long breath. "Not sure. Sawyer does all the hiring and I trust him. I'm concerned if you do that, then that will undermine our relationship."

"Let me know when—"

"Tremblay, you in here?" Fisher's loud voice boomed in the stable.

"Over here." Izzy set her pitchfork aside and waved. "What's going on?"

Fisher kicked at a stack of loose hay. "House is clear to enter now. Forensics just left." He acknowledged Austin. "We'll inform you of what we find."

"Thank you."

"I'd like to check your video footage. Do we have your permission to do that?"

Austin stole a peek at Izzy and raised his eyebrow, waiting to see if she'd respond.

She caught his gesture and cleared her throat. "Fisher, you okay if I do that?"

He placed his hands on his hips. "You think that's wise?"

She smirked. "No, but I know the ranch better than the rest of the force. Or, we could look at it together."

"Well, from what I understand, the mayor is out for your head. You need to be cautious on getting involved." Fisher shifted his glance to Austin. "You good if we look at it together? As much as I give Tremblay a hard time, I'd hate for her to get in trouble."

"Appreciate you looking after her." He hung the pitchforks on their wall hooks. "Let's go to my office."

"I'll tell Mom and Blaire that they can go back to bed." Izzy tucked her hat back on. "I'll meet you there."

Five minutes later the trio hovered around Austin's computer screen. Névé lay on her mat in the office's corner, snoozing. Seemed saving the day had worn his dog out. He thanked God again for keeping them all safe.

Austin adjusted the footage's time to a few minutes before midnight and hit play. "I'm guessing whoever cut the fence did it shortly after midnight because it was around 1:00 a.m. when Névé woke me." Austin pointed to the monitor on the right. "Fisher, you watch this screen. We have six cameras on the property, so three will show here and three on the other. Izzy, keep your eyes peeled on the left monitor."

They studied the video in split screen mode, revealing all angles of the ranch. Except for the blind spot.

"Look here." Izzy pointed to the video covering the property's south side next to the K-9 building.

A blurred image in black splashed gasoline on the walls of the building, scratched a match to life, and then tossed it against one wall, keeping his head concealed. Immediately, flames ignited.

Fisher leaned closer. "Rewind for a few seconds."

Austin obeyed.

"Stop there." Fisher tapped the screen. "See how he looks down? He knows a camera is watching."

Austin pounded the desk. "So, it was an inside job."

"Do you recognize anything about the perp's body language?" Fisher rubbed his chin.

Austin once again rewound the tape and hit play, studying the person closely. He let it play out until the suspect disappeared from the frame. "It could be any of my crew."

"Or someone else entirely." Izzy pulled up a chair. "Let's check out the rest of the footage."

The group examined the videos, even after Maverick, Sawyer and the crew arrived on the scene.

"Do you think it's odd Maverick got there first?" Izzy tapped his desk. "You and Sawyer knew about the fire first, and then you sounded your alarm."

Austin cracked his knuckles before massaging his palms. "Well, his cabin is the closest to the kennels and when I questioned him, he said he smelled the smoke and immediately took action."

Fisher put his hat on. "Looks like a dead end. Gotta get back to work." He waved on his way out of the office.

Izzy nudged Austin. "Okay, let me sit. I want to do a deep dive in your security system to see if someone hacked in."

Austin stood and let her sit in his chair, observing how quickly her fingers flew across his keyboard before the code appeared on his screen. "Wow, that was fast. I forgot how good you are with computers."

"I've loved to push buttons ever since I was a little girl, so I guess it comes naturally." She waved toward the door. "Can you get me a coffee? There's no going back to bed for me now."

"You got it." Austin left and threw a pod into the coffee maker. After fixing it the way Izzy liked it, he entered his office and set it in front of her. "Here you go."

She took a sip. "Aww, that's better. Thanks." She set the cup down and continued clicking on keys.

Seconds later she straightened in her seat, her hand hovering over her mug. "Whoa. This guy is good."

"What do you see?"

She tapped her index finger on a branch of codes. "Hacker's signature."

"What does that mean?"

"Someone got into your system. Most hackers are narcissistic and love to leave a bit of code to mark that they've been in someone's system."

Austin plunked into his chair. "So, maybe not a member of my crew."

If the hacker breached his security system, what else did they do?

Constable Isabelle Tremblay tugged on her police uniform, took a huge breath and walked into the Harturn River Library's conference room. Time to face her accusers and help defend her leader. She placed her hand on her chest, willing her rapid heartbeat to subside. *Stay calm. You've got this.*

Austin had driven her into town along with Névé and planned on taking his dog for a walk in a nearby park while Izzy met with the board. He prayed for her before she went inside. While thankful for his support, Izzy still wondered about God's path for her life. She had made a commitment to Him in her teenage years after getting in trouble with her father when she'd made bad friend choices, but lately God seemed to have hidden His plan for her life. Wasn't He listening anymore?

Izzy set aside the question and advanced farther into the room.

Chief Constable Halt approached. "Morning. You okay? I heard from Fisher what happened overnight. You must be exhausted."

"I'll be fine. Thankfully, the four cups of coffee have given me some energy. Plus, knowing I have to defend myself here has kicked in my adrenaline. Trust me, I'm wide awake."

Doug hurried to join them. "Izzy, don't worry. We've got your back. And yours too, Chief Constable Halt."

"Thank you. He's right. We'll defend your actions. I've already met with the board regarding mine. Have you remembered anything more about those missing three hours?"

Izzy pinched the bridge of her nose. "Not really, but we now know Dad used the book cipher for his code, but I haven't figured out the reference book yet. Too many other happenings have interrupted my thoughts."

"Understood. It will come." Halt gestured toward a chair facing the group gathered. "The mayor wants you front and center."

She gritted her teeth. "Let's get this over with."

Before she could sit, her uncle grazed her arm. "Izzy, just be honest, and the group will understand." He leaned closer. "Well, most of them. I don't trust these characters." He rushed to take his seat.

What did that mean? Her mysterious uncle continued to baffle Izzy. She shook her head, sat in her appointed chair and waited for the mayhem to begin.

Mayor Georgia Fox stood and cleared her throat. "Looks like we're all here, so let's get started." She walked to the front of the group. "Thank you for coming on such short notice, but as you know, I received an anonymous tip that needs to be handled immediately."

Izzy gazed at the crowd, noting the board members present, her partner, chief constable, and other coworkers.

Mayor Fox brought out her tablet from her bag and swiped the screen. "Constable Tremblay, here's what your accuser said and I quote, 'Constable Tremblay has been secretly investigating her father's supposed murder on company time, using police resources, and even disguised herself to come to the station when she was told to stay away. It's her fault the station was bombed. And… Chief Constable Halt sanctioned it all. I'm calling for his resignation or I will go public with this knowledge. Then see what Harturn River residents say. Your choice.'"

Izzy's muscles tightened. While she was investigating her father's death, she had not used police resources or done it on duty. Who had accused her? She noted each board member carefully. Was it one of them or perhaps a coworker? She and Fisher didn't always get along, but would he do this? Probably not. The rest of the constables had always been nice to her, so no, it couldn't be them. And why attack their leader? He was always fair to everyone.

Georgia slid the tablet back into her briefcase. "I realize our meeting here may be unorthodox, but after discussing it with the executive board last night, we wanted all of you to hear this at once." She circled Izzy. "What do you have to say for yourself, Constable Tremblay?"

Doug shot to his feet and raised his right hand. "Mayor Fox, sorry for interrupting, but can I say something?"

Georgia flattened her lips, clearly not impressed by his interruption. "Go ahead."

He walked to the front of the room and stood beside Izzy, smiling, before turning to face the group. "Mayor Fox and board members, you will find no finer officer than Constable Isabelle Tremblay. Yes, she may irritate some by her forthwith attitude and determination."

The group laughed.

Doug raised his index finger. "But she gets the job done and crosses no lines she shouldn't. I stand behind and beside my partner. I was the one who agreed to let her come in disguise to the station. Chief Constable Halt and I required her presence in the interview, hoping it would jog her missing three hours of memory."

Board member Vincent Jackson rose to his feet. "Wait, wait. Your father told me about your impeccable memory and that it has helped solve many cases. You're missing three hours?"

Izzy changed her position. "Yes, I was attacked two nights ago, and I believe details in those missing memories will help solve Dad's murder."

Her uncle Ford stood. "My brother died of a heart attack, and I'm tired of you thinking otherwise."

Once again, Izzy stiffened.

Halt stood. "With all due respect, Ford, while we can't comment on an ongoing investigation, we now agree with Constable Tremblay. There's something suspicious about her father's—your brother's—death. She did not use company resources or investigate while on shift. I also stand by my decision to allow her to come to the station. The bomb was not her fault, and I want to know exactly who this accuser is, Mayor Fox."

She raised both hands. "I honestly don't know. Someone delivered the letter to my office by courier and signed it 'concerned citizen.' But even if I knew, I wouldn't reveal a source." She paused. "Unless, of course, you had a warrant."

Izzy adjusted the tight bun at the back of her head and stood. Time to address the group. She had to choose her words wisely, as this board was known for its stern consequences for those they deem rule breakers. Her leader's reputation was at stake. "Good morning, Mayor Fox and board members. First, I want to thank Chief Constable Halt and Constable Carver for their support. I'm not sure who would accuse me of not abiding by the rules, but I promise you, I didn't break any while on duty." She flexed her hands, attempting to curb the anger rising toward her accuser. "But yes, this person is correct about a couple of things. I looked into my dad's death because it wasn't an accident." She took a second and stared at her uncle.

His stoic expression conveyed his thoughts. He was not happy with her.

She ignored him and continued. "As you know, I have hyperthymesia and what that means is I can recall things in detail. My father showed me his blood work from his annual physical and told me everything the doctor said. We had a very close relationship." She pushed back the tears threatening to rise. "I remember the conversation vividly. He was in perfect health. Somehow someone got to him and caused his accident." Once again, she paused for effect. "Wouldn't you each want to know if *your* loved one was murdered?"

Murmurs filled the room as the attendees whispered to each other.

Mayor Fox banged her palm on a nearby table. "Order!"

The group silenced.

"We already know I disguised myself to be present in the interrogation room while a suspect was being interviewed." She walked to the right side of the room and turned. "My father's CI had contacted me about a key component of whatever case Dad had been working on. For some reason, it was top secret. Not sure why. I agreed to meet with the CI, but someone attacked us. He was killed, and they hit me on the back of my head. That's what caused me to block out three hours of my memory, so I had to find out what happened during that window. It's vital to solving my father's murder."

Vincent raised his hand. "Did it help you remember?"

"Only a bit. Still lots missing, unfortunately."

The man leaned back in his chair, folding his arms. "Well, I, for one, understand why you did what you did."

Others nodded.

Mayor Fox cleared her throat. "Okay, do you have anything else to add before the board convenes to make a decision, Constable Tremblay?"

Izzy stared at her leader. What more could she say to protect the man from whatever penalty the board would dish out? "Only that I beg you not to punish Chief Constable Halt for my actions. If you want to suspend me, go ahead, but he did nothing wrong. He was just placing his trust in one of his officers." She scanned each of the board members' faces. "Most of you knew my father. He had an impeccable track record and was a man of integrity. Don't tarnish that reputation now by punishing someone he trained from the ground up. Plus don't you want his killer to be found? I know I do." She smiled and sat.

Mayor Fox spoke to the group. "This meeting is adjourned. Since I have another pressing matter to attend to, the board will meet tomorrow morning to make our decision. Dismissed."

Izzy quickly texted "done" to Austin. All she wanted to do now was get back to the ranch and once again study her father's codes. Maybe being away from the pages for a few hours had helped clear her mind.

"Good job, partner." Doug squeezed her shoulder.

Halt approached. "I want you to know that whatever happens is not your fault." He waggled his finger at her. "Got it?"

She saluted. "Yes, sir." Her cell phone dinged. Text from Austin.

Névé and I are in the car, ready to take you home.

Wait, did he just say home?

She reread his message and drew in a sharp breath.

He did.

"What is it?"

"Nothing, Chief Constable." She tucked her phone away. "I'm sorry about all this."

"You best get going." He glanced right, then left, before leaning closer. "I want you back safe at the ranch."

"Heading there now." She turned to Doug. "Call with updates, okay?"

Her partner nodded. "Stay off the grid."

She knew what that meant. Disconnect from any computers. But how could she do that when a killer was still on the loose?

Austin turned right onto the secondary road, leading away from Harturn River. He'd chosen the less traveled route. Drivers used the divided highway, but Austin preferred the countryside drive. "How did it go? You've been quiet ever since we left the library."

"Sorry, I'm just upset about the whole thing. I get why Mayor Fox has to investigate the claim. It's part of her job, but this is a man's reputation at stake."

"Yours too. Surely the board will side with you."

"I tried to appeal to their emotions, but my uncle is still mad at me and he has a loud voice, so to speak." She huffed. "The others will listen to him."

"Let's pray that doesn't happen."

"I want to know who sent the allegations to the mayor. Apparently, the anonymous note was delivered to her office by courier." She yawned. "I want to get back to the ranch and focus on Dad's message. Plus I'm growing used to the serenity there."

Névé barked from her kennel in the back.

Austin chuckled. "She enjoys having you." And so did he, but he wouldn't voice that thought.

The malamute barked again, then growled.

Austin's pulse elevated. He trusted his K-9's instincts. Something else had caught her attention.

"What is it, girl?" He checked the rearview mirror. It was then he noticed a delivery truck approaching at full speed. "Not good."

"What?" Izzy turned and cried out. "He's coming fast!"

"Hang on." Austin gripped the wheel of his SUV and stepped on the accelerator.

The vehicle swerved on the icy road, and he fought to maintain control.

Izzy pounded on the dash. "He's gonna ram us!"

Seconds later the truck smashed into their bumper, shoving the SUV forward over the double-line road.

The wheels hit a patch of ice and spun the vehicle.

Izzy screamed.

Névé barked.

Austin prayed.

He compensated and yanked the wheel, righting the vehicle once again.

But the driver didn't stop. The truck hit them again, sending them toward the embankment at full speed.

Lord, save us!

The SUV launched over the ditch, plowed into a mound of snow and crashed into a tree.

The airbags deployed as Austin's head whacked against the cushioned steering wheel.

Pain registered as the impact sent an explosion of spots flickering in his vision moments before the darkness sucked him under.

THIRTEEN

Izzy jerked awake, pain piercing her right arm as confusion plagued her mind. Where was she? How long had she been unconscious? A barking dog registered, and she turned, noting Austin's face buried in the airbag. She unfastened her seat belt and inched closer, wincing from the pain in her arm. She pulled his head away from the wheel, using her left hand. "Austin!" She checked his pulse. Steady.

He was alive but out cold.

Once again, Névé barked while she scratched at her cage, as if she knew her master was in trouble.

Izzy withdrew her cell phone from her coat pocket and hit 911, praying her signal was at least strong enough to call for help. "Come on. Work for me." *Please, Lord.*

The operator answered and inquired about her emergency.

She identified herself as a police officer, naming her badge. "Car accident. Possible suspect still in the area. Male in his early thirties is unconscious. Need an ambulance and backup at my location." She named the road, mile marker and the delivery truck's license plate number. She included the model and color.

"You positive about that information?"

Izzy had read it moments before the truck hit them. "Absolutely."

"Can you get out of the vehicle?"

She had to. Austin's life was on the line. "I'm going to try. Get help here fast."

"They're on their way."

Izzy punched off the call and took in her surroundings. The darkened interior obstructed her view out the front windshield.

She looked right, then left. The entire front of the vehicle was buried in snow.

Mounds of snow.

Their only escape route was through the back. But how could she get Austin to safety? Her wounded arm prevented her from being able to get him out quickly. A vision of Névé hauling Goose from the burning building formed in her mind.

Névé could do it. Malamutes could haul lots of weight, but first Izzy had to get to her and clear a path out through the back. She turned in her seat. Another stab of pain stopped her in her tracks. She grasped her arm, sucking in a ragged breath. Her pulse elevated at her sudden action. *Slow movements, Iz. You can do this. You* have *to do this.*

Izzy didn't know if the vehicle would blow. She had to get them all out now. She couldn't lose Austin. Again.

And Névé too.

She breathed in. Out. In. Out. Her heartbeat slowed. "Okay, girl. I'm coming to you. We have to get Austin out."

Névé barked.

First, Izzy reached over Austin and hit the button to release the Expedition's tailgate. It popped open and cold air snaked into the vehicle. She ignored the chill, put her seat down and gingerly crawled into the back. Pulling on the passenger side right lever, she flattened the seat. Then did the same to the left. She wiggled over to the driver's side and reached around to bring Austin's seat as far back as it would go. Once again, she winced from the pain throbbing in her arm.

"Time to get you out of your kennel." Izzy inched into the back and pushed the tailgate open the rest of the way, then unfastened Névé's kennel door. There was just enough room on the crate's other side for the dog to bring Austin through the back. "Okay, girl, we need to do this together. I'm counting on your strength."

Woof! The dog nestled close.

Izzy kissed Névé's forehead. "Okay, what's the command for you to tug Austin out?" Izzy searched her mind looking for the answer, but Austin never gave the malamute such a command. She'd have to wing it. "I'm going back up front to help."

Izzy crawled toward Austin's driver's seat and unfastened his seat belt. "Austin, this would be easier if you just woke up! Please."

The only sound came from Névé's panting.

Izzy patted the console. "Névé, come."

The dog obeyed, crawling in between the two front seats.

With her left arm, Izzy hauled Austin to the right toward his dog. She drew his zipper down from his neck, then lifted his hood. "Névé, mush!" She took a hunch on the command since she knew malamutes pulled sleds.

Instantly, the dog latched on to Austin's hood and tugged backward.

Using her left hand, Izzy helped ease Austin from his position enough so his dog could pull him out through the Expedition's back. She crawled alongside the dog, interjecting to ensure Austin wouldn't hit his head. "You've got this, Névé. Keep pulling."

Finally, the malamute hauled Austin to the edge of the tailgate. "Névé, stop!"

Izzy couldn't have her dropping Austin out of the vehicle. She had to protect his head, but it would be a challenge for her to get over the crate and Austin.

She held her breath, anticipating the throbbing pain in her arm would increase, then pushed the crate to a different angle. She shimmied her way through and hopped out the back.

"Okay, Névé, down." Izzy tucked her arms beneath Austin's shoulders. *This is gonna hurt, Iz.* But she couldn't risk Austin bumping his head, and she needed to get him out of the vehicle.

Névé leaped from the tailgate.

Izzy gently brought Austin out, ignoring the fire burning in her arm. She set him in the snow. "Névé, mush!" She pointed toward a tree.

Once again, the malamute clamped on to Austin's hood and dragged him over to where Izzy had indicated.

Izzy followed and ruffled the dog's head. "You're such a smart dog."

Névé snuggled next to Austin, licking his face. Her form of CPR?

Izzy smiled and plunked herself beside him, glancing back at his Expedition. They had plowed into a mound of snow before hitting the tree. The snow from the enormous birch tree must have fallen on top, completing the burial. Thankfully, the back end had escaped the white grave. *Thank You, Lord, for helping us get out.*

She focused on Austin and nudged him. "Austin, can you hear me? Wake up!"

Nothing.

She caressed his face. "Come back to me." Izzy leaned down and kissed his forehead, letting her lips linger for a second. "I miss you," she whispered. All she wanted to do right now was bring him into her arms and hold tight. He had always confessed to being her protector, but now the tables were turned.

Time for Constable Tremblay to protect her long-lost friend. She harrumphed. Who was she kidding? The emotions resurfacing were for more than a friend. Dare she open her heart again? Or would he reject her like he had after Clara's death, abandoning their friendship?

No, she couldn't risk the pain, especially after dating Dax. The man's obsessiveness forced her to end things, breaking her heart just after opening it again. Their relationship had ended with her taking out a restraining order against him.

Even though Izzy knew Austin wasn't Dax, he had deserted her in her hour of need.

Névé growled, pulling her from past regrets.

Izzy froze.

Movement from the road caught her attention, and she flew to her feet, whirling around.

A flash of a figure dressed in white appeared in her peripheral vision moments before a shotgun blast boomed.

Izzy threw herself on top of Austin and Névé, shielding them with her body.

Pain exploded in her arm.

Sirens sounded in the distance. Help was coming.

But would it arrive too late?

Austin struggled to wake up and move his body as tightness seized his chest. He fought to clear his dazed brain. Sirens blared in the background, followed by a dog barking. Why did his head hurt so much? Something shifted on top of him and the pressure eased. Névé licked his face. The crash! *Austin, wake up. Izzy could be hurt.* He willed himself to rise, but his body wouldn't listen.

"Austin! Wake up. We need to take shelter."

Izzy's panicked voice cut through Austin's fog, jolting him awake. He opened his eyes.

Névé's face appeared inches away from him. Obviously, the dog wanted her handler to wake up too.

"Izzy, are you okay?" Austin's question came out in a squeak. He cleared his throat and eased upward. "Where are we?"

"Stay down for a moment." Izzy pushed on his shoulders. "We're under attack. One shot fired. Help is on the way."

Austin rubbed his head. "I must have whacked my head good."

"Can you move? We have to get behind the tree."

"Yes, but I need help to get up." He grabbed her right arm. She cried out.

He hesitated. "Sorry. Are you hurt?"

"Slammed into the armrest upon impact, but I believe it's only sprained."

A chill snaked down the back of his neck not only from the rush of cold air, but the thought of Izzy getting hurt. He observed the vehicle. "How did you get me out?"

She pointed to Névé. "With help from a furry friend."

Austin braced himself and pushed upward. "Good girl." He patted her head.

The malamute barked and hopped up on all fours.

Angst bombarded Austin, and he changed his position to protect Névé. "Is the shooter still out there, Iz?"

"I don't think so. Probably heard the approaching sirens and fled." She brushed the snow from her uniform. "Let's get behind the tree, just in case."

Austin pushed himself up and scrambled to hide with Izzy and Névé. He glanced around the tree and once again studied his Ford buried in the snow. He guessed the front end was probably demolished from the impact. *Thank You, Father, for saving us.* "Iz, did you catch the truck's license plate number with your sharp memory?"

"Sure did and gave it to the 911 operator." She brought out her phone. "Going to call Doug." She hit a button and put the call on speakerphone.

"Izzy, you okay? We're almost at your location." Doug's frantic voice crackled in the limited cell reception.

"Minor injuries. I gave the truck's license plate number to the 911 operator, but I'll text it to you, too."

The loud sirens announced the arrival of emergency services. An ambulance, fire truck and police cruiser pulled to the side of the road.

"I'm here now, but yes, text it to me. We'll get on it. Another cruiser is searching the area for the truck." A car door slamming came through Doug's phone as the connection severed.

Izzy tapped on her screen before pocketing her phone and turning to Austin. "I need to tell you something. The delivery truck had King & Sons on the side. I failed to mention that to the operator as I was in a bit of a hurry to get help, but wanted you to know."

"Them again." He sighed. "You still think Sawyer is involved?"

Doug's head appeared over the embankment. "Izzy, Austin, where are you?"

"I'm not sure who to trust anymore, but Sawyer seems to be on the up-and-up. I don't think the King in the name is any relation to him." Izzy stood and waved. "Over here."

Austin brought himself upright and leaned against the tree for support. His shaky legs told him he required rest. The previous adrenaline from a night of chaos had left his body after the crash.

Doug maneuvered down the embankment, gun in hand. "Did you see the shooter?"

"Only quickly." Izzy pointed to the right. "I saw the suspect run that way, dressed in white. I'm guessing to camouflage in the snow."

Austin massaged the growing bump on his forehead. "They must have followed us from the library, but I took alternative routes and didn't catch a tail. I made sure of it. The truck came out of nowhere."

Izzy's jaw dropped. "Doug, do you think this whole accusation was a ruse to get me out of hiding? Whoever it was understood police business and also knew we'd be there."

"What do you mean?" A gust of icy wind sent chills down Austin's neck. He zipped his coat.

"That if they implicated Chief Constable Halt's decision in my conduct, I would come to defend him."

Doug tapped his temple. "Smart thinking."

Austin noticed the paramedics trudging through the snow. "They knew where the meeting was being held. The suspect has to be someone you know well, or maybe someone on the force, or who attended the meeting."

"It's not one of us." Doug's radio crackled, but the caller's words were broken. "Come again."

"No. Sign of. Suspect."

"Copy that. Keep looking. They couldn't have gotten too far on foot." Doug holstered his weapon. "Listen, you guys get checked out and then if the paramedics clear you, I'll take you back to the ranch." He focused on Izzy. "In the meantime, I'll get started on checking into the truck and I'll take your statements at Austin's place."

Izzy cradled her right arm, using her left hand. "Have the team dig deeper into King & Sons as it was their delivery truck that rammed us. I want to know who they are and what they deliver. Unfortunately, I haven't had time to look into them."

Austin noted the tension in her voice.

Whoever had steamrolled them off the road was about to face the wrath of Constable Isabelle Tremblay.

Not that Austin blamed her. This had to end before anyone else got hurt—or killed.

FOURTEEN

Later that afternoon, after getting cleared by the paramedics and resting, Izzy arranged the second set of prints on her evidence board after she made copies. She didn't trust that whoever was trying to kill them wouldn't find out about her secret copy. She fingered the sling, protecting her right arm. Her sprain would heal in time. *Guess I won't be going back to work anytime soon.* Although, her father had taught her to shoot using both hands.

The paramedics had taken Austin to the hospital to be examined by a doctor. Thankfully, he only had a mild concussion, and the doctor sent him home with instructions. When they had arrived back at the ranch, Sawyer hovered around his friend to make sure Austin obeyed the doctor's orders.

Dr. Gardner had checked Névé over and gave her a clean bill of health, so Austin gave his dog multiple treats for hauling him from the vehicle.

Izzy gazed at the malamute sleeping in the corner. Tears formed as she thought about having to leave once this case was solved. She squeezed the bridge of her nose, willing her emotions to remain at bay. *I'll miss you, sweet girl.*

She tucked regrets away and picked up the tape to add the last page to the board.

"Why aren't you resting?" Blaire shuffled into the room.

Izzy startled from her sister's stealth-like approach. "You scared me. Blaire, I need to get answers and they're here in Dad's secret code."

"Weren't you just at a meeting because you're involved in a case you shouldn't be?"

Izzy didn't miss the hostile tone in her question. "I'm on vacation and not using company resources. Don't you *want* to find out what really happened to Dad?"

"How many times do we have to tell you? It was an accident. Uncle Ford says—"

"What's with you and Uncle Ford lately? It's like you're two peas in a pod."

Blaire's eyes clouded. "He was there when I needed him. He listened and didn't judge me."

Izzy dropped the tape. "What are you referring to? Have I offended you? You haven't seemed to be yourself lately."

Blaire took two long strides forward and waggled her finger in Izzy's face. "You know exactly. Luca and I were in love, and you wrecked everything."

Izzy's jaw dropped. "He was married and a suspect in a child's abduction! I only wanted to protect you."

"No, you and your holier-than-thou attitude judged me. Luca and his wife were getting a divorce."

"Do you really believe that? If that's the case, why were they still together?" Izzy crossed her arms. "When we went to the house the day of his child's abduction, he and his wife certainly didn't look like they were on the outs. In fact, Luca said he'd been on the phone planning a ceremony to renew their vows when his daughter was taken."

"You're lying!" Blaire's voice raised a notch.

Névé hopped up on all fours.

"Be quiet. Austin is resting down the hall." Izzy caressed her sister's arm. "I'm sorry for everything you've been through with Luca, but I never judged you. I've made my own mistakes with Dax."

She jerked her arm away. "Well, Luca told me you're the reason he broke up with me."

Izzy stumbled backward. "What? That's absurd. Why would he say that?"

"He said he couldn't date someone whose sister thought he was guilty." A tear fell down her cheek. "That's why he's still with his wife."

Izzy blew out a breath. When would her sister acknowledge Luca's lies? He probably never loved her. However, Izzy would keep that thought to herself. Her relationship with Blaire was already on shaky ground. "I realize it's hard, but it's time to move on. Please trust me when I say I never meant to hurt you. I'm sorry that I obviously did, and hope one day you can forgive me." Once again, she grazed Blaire's arm. "I miss you. We used to tell each other our deepest secrets and fears. We haven't done that in a long time."

Blaire jerked away from Izzy's touch. "Well, I'm not ready to forgive and forget." She stomped out of the room.

Izzy plopped into the desk chair, burying her head in her hands. *Lord, I'm not sure if You're listening, but can You bring my sister back to me? We need each other.*

"You okay, Iz?" Austin's softened voice revealed his concern.

She popped her head up. "Sorry if Blaire's yelling woke you. I'm frustrated. My sister seems to hate me and claims I interfered with her and Luca's relationship." She leaned back, folding her arms. "I just wish she could see his lies."

"I'm sorry she feels that way. I'm here if you want to talk."

"Appreciate that." Izzy always loved their conversations and missed his friendship. "How are you feeling?"

"Still have a bit of a headache, but not bad." He pointed to the evidence board. "I see you have the copies back up. Any headway?"

"I'm afraid not."

Austin advanced farther into his office and bent to pet Névé on his way to the board. "Good girl, keeping Iz company."

The dog snuggled into Austin and licked his face.

"Aw, I love that she loves you so much." Izzy stood and walked to the board, studying each number. "I wish I could figure out Dad's reference book. I have so many, and I'm not sure which one he would have picked."

Austin positioned himself beside Izzy, his woodsy scent wafting into her space.

Don't do that to me.

It was getting harder and harder to keep herself from falling for this man a second time.

Who was she kidding? It only took seeing him again for those emotions to return.

He tapped one sheet. "Wait, these numbers in the top corner kind of resemble a date."

Izzy abandoned thoughts of Austin and peered closer. "You're right. It does. How did I miss that?"

"Well, it's squished together. Perhaps your dad tried to disguise it from prying eyes. So what happened on October 3, 2000? Wait, October 3 is your birthday. Did you get something special that day?"

Izzy searched her memory bank and inhaled audibly. "Yes, it was the birthday he gave me my first Nancy Drew book. *The Hidden Staircase*. That's it! That has to be the reference book."

"Do you have that book at your condo?"

"Yes. I need to go get it."

Her mother shuffled into the room. "You're not going anywhere. When will you realize someone is trying to kill you?"

Izzy pivoted and faced her mother. "Well, I need a book from my condo."

Her mother swiped the screen on her cell phone. "I'll get Ford to pick it up and bring it."

Izzy's gaze snapped to Austin's. She raised a brow, silently pleading for help.

She didn't want her uncle involved. Something irritated her about his actions lately. She only wished she understood why.

Austin gave her a slight nod and placed his hand over top of Izzy's mother's. "Rebecca, Sawyer is heading out for a run of dog food anyway. I'll get him to swing by." He turned to Izzy. "That okay with you?"

"Of course. I'll give you my key."

"Fine. Don't accept my help. Again." Her mother marched out of the room.

How many times would a family member leave the room angry with Izzy today?

Izzy withdrew her keys from her purse and handed them to Austin. "Sorry about that. Not sure why my family seems to have it in for me right now. I'm just trying to find out the truth."

"No need to apologize. I'll get Sawyer on it right away, so you can get started on decoding the message." He took a step, but turned. "Wait, where would the book be?"

"In my office. However, he'll have to search through them because the perp tossed all my books on the floor and I haven't been back to clean them up." She raised her finger. "But I'll get Doug to meet him there. I don't want Sawyer to go in unprotected. Padilla or his men may still stake out my condo. Plus I need to see if he has any updates."

"Good plan." Austin left the room.

Izzy sat back at her desk and punched in her partner's number.

He answered on the second ring. "Hey, you. Was just gonna call you. I have news."

"Good, and I have a favor to ask." She explained the situation.

"No problem. I can do that." The rustling of papers sounded through the phone. "So, no prints found on the jerrican."

"No surprise there. It's winter, and the perp would have worn gloves anyway. What else?"

"We did a thorough analysis into King & Sons. We know it's a shell corporation, but the team discovered something very interesting."

Izzy sat straighter in her chair, anticipating some good news. The cheerful tone in her partner's voice was a dead giveaway. She hoped. "What did they find?"

"Sawyer is on his way to your condo," Austin said, stepping into the room. He halted. "Sorry for interrupting."

"No worries." Izzy picked up a pen and tapped the desk. "Doug was sharing what he found out about King & Sons. I'll put you on speaker, Doug."

"Hey, Austin. I'm heading to Izzy's condo as soon as I'm off the phone." A chair scraping sounded through the phone.

"Appreciate your protection for Sawyer." Austin sat at his desk.

"No problem," Doug said. "Izzy, to answer your question, King & Sons delivers kitchen equipment and specializes in fixing burners."

Izzy sprang to her feet. "As in burners that could be used for cooking drugs?"

"Possibly. That's our guess too. Here's the interesting part. We linked the company to none other than our honorable mayor."

"What? Oh, that just takes the cake." Was Georgia responsible for the supposed accusations against them?

"Well, let's not jump to conclusions. Could be someone trying to implicate her. She's ruffled feathers to get into office. We're still looking into it."

Izzy sat back down. "Thanks for the update."

"Sorry it's not more."

"Well, it's better than nothing. I'm hoping once I decode Dad's message, I'll have information for you."

A squawking radio sailed through the speakerphone. "Just a sec, Izzy. I'm getting an update."

Izzy tensed, waiting to hear if it had to do with her father's case.

Muffled voices sounded in the background.

"Izzy, I just learned that someone killed Bolton and Phillips in jail," Doug's voice blared.

"What?" A realization dawned on Izzy.

They would never be safe from Padilla if they didn't soon find answers to the missing pieces of her perfect memory. Somehow, they held the key.

Austin returned to his office forty minutes after ensuring the ranch's perimeter was still secure.

Izzy stood motionless in front of her evidence board.

Exactly where he'd left her. *Lord, show her the hidden message.*

Austin inched into the room, stopping to pet Névé, who continued to stay with Izzy. "You're a good girl."

Izzy spun around. "Sorry, didn't hear you come in."

Austin handed her a cup of coffee. "Sawyer back yet?"

"No. I've been studying the numbers and other pages of the journal, trying to make sense of it all." She pointed to two pages on the board. "These numbers are different and follow the same format as my birth date clue."

Austin got up and positioned himself beside her. "So, more dates, but dates of what?"

"I'm thinking drug deals, perhaps? These two pages came before the coded ones. Not sure if that's significant or not."

He breathed in, soaking up his closeness to her as he realized it would end soon and she'd be out of his life forever.

And that thought scared him to the core.

Since she'd been thrust back into his life, he realized he didn't want to let her go again.

Did she feel the same?

Austin's gaze locked with hers. He caressed her cheek. "Iz, I—"

"I'm back!" Sawyer's booming voice sounded from the hallway.

Austin cleared his throat and stepped backward moments before his friend entered the room.

Sawyer raised the book. "Got it." He handed it to Izzy.

"Thanks." She cradled the book as if it were a child. "Did you have any issues at the condo?"

"No, your partner cleared the house before I went in." He whistled. "Quite the mess in your office."

"I know. I hate not being able to go clean it up, but I can't take the risk of Padilla's men following me there again." Izzy opened the book and sat at her desk.

"Alrighty then. I'm off to fix the fence." Sawyer spoke to Austin. "I hope you're okay with this, but I picked up surveillance equipment for the blind spot while I was out. Maverick and I are going to hook it up now before supper."

Austin locked his arms at his sides. "Do you trust him, Sawyer? I know you did a reference check on him, but he acts suspiciously around me."

"He doesn't with me. Perhaps your police spidey senses are misfiring."

"Maybe. Just monitor him. Thanks for installing the camera."

"No prob." Sawyer left the room.

"Iz, I changed my mind." Austin rolled his desk chair over beside her. "Can you get Doug to look into Maverick? I need to know he's okay, especially with everything that's been happening."

"Sure. I'll text him right now." Izzy keyed on her cell phone. "Okay, done. Time to work on decoding Dad's hidden message. Wanna help?"

"Absolutely."

"You read out the numbers and I'll check the book. Let's hope this is the correct edition." Izzy hopped up and yanked the printout from the board. She handed it to Austin before sitting. "Okay, ready."

Thirty minutes later, after false and frustrating leads, Izzy slammed her hand on the desk. "That's it! The first set of numbers is longitude and latitude."

Austin rolled his chair over to his desk and grabbed his laptop. "We can see it on the map better using my laptop. Give me the numbers."

She spieled them off.

Austin typed them in and immediately a map appeared on his screen. He enlarged it.

And drew in a sharp breath.

"What is it?" Izzy shot out of her chair and peered over Austin's shoulder.

He pointed. "That location isn't far from here, but it's a secluded wilderness. What would we be looking for?"

Izzy picked up the printout. "Wait, there's more numbers on the bottom. Maybe a second clue?"

She snatched the book and relocated to the evidence board. "Read them out to me."

He said each one slowly, allowing time for her to look up the words.

She wrote them on the board one at a time, then stood back.

Austin studied her father's additional message.

Tall, Behind, Secret, Trees, Entrance, Cellar.

"That's a jumbled mess." Austin tilted his head, observing each word separately. "What does it mean?"

"Dad and I liked to play this game. Figure out the message in the scrambled words." Izzy chewed on the end of the marker.

Seconds later her eyes widened, and she frantically wrote the secret message below the words:

Secret cellar entrance behind tall trees.

"That's it! Dad found something in the forest. A building." She snagged her cell phone from the desk. "We need to go look. Now!"

"Shouldn't you call Doug?" Austin didn't like that she'd put herself at risk so quickly after being run off the road.

"Good point." She punched in his number and waited. "No

answer. I'll leave a message." She gave Doug the details before hanging up. "Are you okay to go?" She snatched the eraser from the ledge and removed the clues from the board. Just in case.

He clamped his lips shut. Knowing he wouldn't be able to contain her excitement at the thought of perhaps finding a missing piece to the mystery, he willed strength into his body. "I'm good. Let me grab my hunting rifle and a flashlight. If it's a cellar, we'll need the light." He addressed Névé. "Come."

His malamute trotted behind him as a question rose in Austin's mind.

He guessed something sinister lay hidden, or why else would Chief Constable Tremblay go to the trouble of hiding the message?

No, Austin wouldn't go into the wilderness unarmed.

FIFTEEN

Izzy skulked behind a snowcapped fir tree, peering in all directions for any potential suspects. However, the forest remained silent in the late afternoon hour on the frigid winter day. The only sound interrupting the surrounding solitude was Névé's breathing. Both she and Austin stood close, guarding Izzy. Not that she couldn't protect herself, but Austin's rifle gave her peace of mind. She remembered his impeccable aim and took solace in his close presence. She knew he was unhappy with her for not waiting for her partner, but she needed evidence. After all, maybe they had decoded the message incorrectly. Even though she might put her career on the line if the board found out, lives were at stake. The sooner they stopped Padilla, the sooner the community would be safe from both him and his deadly drugs.

Izzy spotted a cluster of tall trees along with two sets of footprints. She pointed. "That could be where Dad found the secret entrance."

Austin raised his rifle. "Let me go first, since you're not armed. Névé, stay." He trudged through the snow, stopping at trees to hide his approach. He reached the group of trees and circled them, searching in various spots. Suddenly he stopped and bent down, brushing off snow from something beneath the bushes. He waved her over.

Izzy and Névé advanced as Austin had. She searched the woods for signs of life and any spying eyes, but found none. She hurried to where Austin stood. "What did you find?"

He pointed to a secret door hidden by a group of bushes. "Exactly where your dad said it would be. You open it. I'll cover you."

Izzy squatted and grasped the handle with her left hand, peering back at Austin. "Just a sec. Why isn't this door locked?"

Austin shrugged. "Perhaps they guessed nobody would find it?" He pushed another branch away. "Wait. There's the chain and lock. Someone obviously forgot to lock up. Careless." He gestured toward multiple tracks around the bushes. "Looks like someone was here recently. Maybe we should get out of here and give Doug the details about the opening."

No way. Izzy's inquisitive mind had to know more before bringing in the team. "I want to check it out quickly first."

He pursed his lips.

"I know what you're thinking. We'll take it slow and if we hear anyone inside, we'll leave. Ready?" She kept her voice low in case there were people behind the door.

He nodded and turned to Névé. "Silence," he whispered.

The malamute raised her nose in the air, standing tall on all fours. Ready for action, but remained quiet.

Izzy tugged the heavy door open. The hinges creaked in annoyance and she winced, holding her breath.

But only a dark stone staircase appeared, leading downward.

Izzy flicked on the flashlight and shone it through the entrance, then turned to Austin. "Let's go together. Slowly."

He dipped his chin in acknowledgment and moved to her side, turning to Névé. "Come."

Izzy guided their way, using the flashlight's beam as they descended. Once at the bottom, she peered left down the only hallway in the hidden cellar.

"Let's see where this leads," she whispered.

They inched their way along the damp corridor walls. Izzy listened for any type of movement, but the cellar remained silent. After a few minutes, they reached a door. She eased it open. "More stairs but going up. Odd."

Another door appeared at the top.

"Let me go first." Austin raised his weapon and advanced through the entry.

Izzy and Névé followed, stepping into a dark room.

"What is this place? We're no longer underground." Izzy shone the flashlight, the beam revealing stone walls of a boarded-up house. "Where are we?"

"This has to be the old Montgomery place. The family moved Mrs. Montgomery to a nursing home years ago, but they never sold the property. Their daughter lives on the other end of the town."

Izzy moved the beam around the room. Rows of tables lined the area. Burners sat on top of each, along with chemicals and gas masks. This had to be where Padilla's men cooked the drugs.

Austin paced the room, feeling around the obscured windows and one door. "Sealed tight. The only way in is the secret cellar entrance."

"No one is here. Let's get a closer look." She shone the flashlight as she approached the nearest table.

A burner marked with King & Sons on the side was placed at one end. A row of small bags on the other. She pointed to the company's logo. "Interesting." She inched closer. Heat radiated from one burner. "Someone was just here. This one is still warm."

"We gotta hurry." Austin pointed to a bag. "I'm guessing this is the bath salts you mentioned." He turned from his position beside her. "Check this out, Iz."

Boxes stacked in the corner reached up to the ceiling. She whistled. "I'm guessing they're getting ready to transport these." She shone the light upward. "Wow, they have an advanced ventilation system. Padilla thought of everything." Izzy handed him the flashlight. "I'm going to take pictures to send to Doug."

"Do it quickly because we can't stay in here long unprotected."

She took out her phone and snapped pictures of everything in the room. Tables full of drugs, burners, various chemicals, glass beakers and multiple boxes. She pocketed her phone. "Okay, let's go."

They retreated out of the room, back down the stairs and up toward the cellar entrance.

Austin moved ahead of her. "Let me go first." He raised his rifle and inched up the stone steps, then through the opening.

Seconds later his face appeared. "It's all clear."

As Izzy stepped into the fresh air, she breathed deeply before studying the forest. All remained quiet. She followed Austin to the clearing.

Névé growled.

Both Izzy and Austin stopped at his dog's warning.

A branch cracked behind them. Someone had entered the forest to the right of their location.

Austin shoved her behind a cluster of trees.

"Bro, check out these footprints," a snarly voice said. "Should we call the boss?"

"Naw. Look at the paw prints. Probably just someone out for a walk in the snowy woods with their dog." The other male voice boomed in the forest. "We don't want him getting mad at us. You remember what happened the last time we were wrong about something? Almost lost our lives. Padilla doesn't play nice, even with his staff."

So this *was* Padilla's cooking lab. Izzy couldn't wait to update Doug.

"Yeah, I remember. Still have the bruise on my face to prove it." He paused. "Let's inspect the area and ensure we're alone. I see prints this way."

Izzy bit the inside of her mouth, waiting for the men to proceed farther into the forest.

"Man, it's snowing again. I don't see anyone. Whoever it was, is gone. Let's get back to work. I don't want to get stuck here again. It's too creepy in that dark house."

"We need to remain hidden. That female cop is getting too close. Our spy is setting it up so she'll be out of the picture soon. Just like her old man."

Izzy bit down hard to keep herself from crying out. *Spy?* She glanced at Austin.

His widened eyes told her he had caught the reference.

Padilla had indeed sent an enemy into their camp.

The question was…who?

Austin entered his office and handed Izzy a cup of orange hot chocolate. He had added whipped cream and dropped miniature marshmallows on top. "Your fave."

She smiled and took a sip. "So good. You remembered."

"Yup, you're not the only one with an excellent memory." He sipped his mug of hot chocolate, the orange flavor lingering on his lips. "Anything from Doug yet?"

She shook her head. "I'm waiting for his call." She plunked herself down behind her desk, placing her cup in front of her. "I miss my dad. He'd know what to do about this case."

Austin set his mug aside and brought her upright into his arms. "I know. I'm sorry. It's hard losing a parent. I lost both of mine at once in a tragic car accident."

"I remember it happened after Clara died. That must have been so hard for you to deal with on top of everything."

She didn't know the half of it. He had longed to reach out to her, but their strained relationship had prevented him from calling. He had caused her too much pain. He released her from his embrace. "Thankfully, Sawyer was working here by then and he was a huge help to me. His faith in God was an inspiration and after long talks, I resurrendered my life to Him."

"Well, God doesn't seem to show me His path for me anymore or be listening to my prayers."

"Sometimes God shows us, but our blinders prevent us from seeing His plan." He paused. "At least, that's what Sawyer said to me."

"My dad used to say something similar, but sometimes life's just too hard." Izzy moved behind her desk and drank more hot chocolate as if wanting to silence their God conversation.

Whipped cream lingered on her top lip, distracting Austin. What would it be like to kiss her? He had wanted to for years, but of course, their working relationship prevented him from disclosing his true feelings for her.

What about now? *Tell her, Austin. Tell her how you really feel.*

Would she abandon him like everyone else had in his life? His biological parents didn't love him enough to keep him. His adoptive parents technically hadn't abandoned him, but their absence in his life was a deep loss. *Why take everyone from me, God?* Every woman he'd dated in the past ten years had left him, stating he couldn't commit.

They weren't wrong. He kept comparing each to Izzy, and even though he tried his hardest to have feelings for them, he just couldn't.

Plus she probably wouldn't forgive him for not saving Clara that night.

No, Austin. Lock away your feelings and throw away the key. She doesn't feel the same.

Time to move on. "You have whipped cream on your lip." He leaned closer and rubbed it away with his thumb, allowing his touch to linger.

A soft gasp escaped her lips, and her eyes locked with his.

Even though his earlier determination to stay away was fresh in his mind, he couldn't help but caress her cheek. "Iz—"

"Don't, Austin." She pulled away.

See, she doesn't feel the same.

Her cell phone rang. "It's Doug." She hit the speakerphone button. "Hey, partner. I'm with Austin."

"Good, I need to talk to you both. Sorry to bother you so late."

Izzy dropped into her chair. "What's going on?"

Doug cleared his throat. "First of all, Izzy, next time you get a lead, wait for me."

She fingered the sling on her right arm. "Doug, I realize I should have waited, but I didn't want you coming all the way out there if the uncoded message was nothing."

"I get it, but you're already in hot water. Anyway. I gave Halt the information, and he's getting a search warrant based on the evidence you provided." He inhaled. "The team will be raiding the cookhouse soon, but you can't be involved."

She slouched. "I get it."

"We've had another teen overdose from the bath salts, so the chief is eager to stop Padilla."

Izzy's hand flew to her mouth. "How old?"

"Fourteen."

"That's three in the last month linked to the drug." Izzy massaged her neck. "No wonder Dad was trying to get to the bottom of the drug ring. I just don't understand why he kept his investigation a secret."

"My guess is because someone higher up the chain is linked to or *is* Padilla." Doug's whispered voice came through the speaker.

Austin guessed the man was struggling to hold his emotions in check.

"You think it may be Mayor Fox?" Izzy rose and walked to the window, peering into the darkness.

"Not saying that and Halt is looking into her connection with King & Sons, but something made your dad write his notes in code."

"Whomever it is, is now targeting Izzy. They silenced her father and now want to do the same to her." Austin noted Izzy's location. "Please get away from the window."

"Another good reason for her to lie low," Doug said. "One more thing. You asked me to look into Maverick. It took some digging, but I found out he was born near Kelowna to a Joyce Shaw and Owen Maynard. Worked on—"

Austin bolted upright. "What?"

Izzy pivoted. "You recognize those names?"

"Yes, they're my biological parents." Realization set in and he stumbled backward. "Maverick is my brother?"

A crash echoed throughout the top level of the ranch house, followed by Blaire's bloodcurdling scream.

SIXTEEN

"Blaire!" Izzy sprang to her feet. "Doug, intruder at Austin's."

"Sending units now." Doug clicked off the call.

Izzy stuffed her phone into her pocket. "Austin, get me one of your rifles and ammo. Blaire's in trouble."

He crouch-walked to his rifle cabinet, punched in a code and removed two, stuffing additional ammo into his pocket. He handed a rifle to Izzy and turned to his dog. "Névé, come."

Izzy checked the chamber before raising her weapon. "Stay behind me and keep low. We don't know what we're dealing with."

"You forget I was your partner once." He tapped his temple. "My police training isn't totally gone from here." He lifted the rifle toward the stairs. "Let's go."

She didn't miss the annoyance in his tone. Was he thinking about their last call together that ended in tragedy? Something told Izzy that Austin wouldn't make the same mistake twice.

At least, she prayed that was the case.

She ignored the trepidation locking her shoulders and crept up the stairs, staying low on the right side of the steps. Even though it hurt to cradle her left hand with her injured right, she continued upward. She wouldn't let her injury cripple her ability to protect her family.

They reached the top of the stairs.

Izzy raced to her sister's room and stopped in front of the closed door, waiting for her ex-partner and his dog.

"Sissy, help!" Her sister's cry turned to muffled screams, as if someone had their hand over her mouth.

Izzy's pulse magnified, sending her into action. She mouthed to Austin, *Ready?*

Austin pressed his back against the wall to the right of the door, flanking her with Névé by his side, and nodded.

Izzy pointed her weapon and pushed the door open. "Police! Stand down."

She moved into the room and stopped in her tracks.

A masked man held a Glock to her sister's temple and grasped his other hand over her mouth.

Tears welled in Blaire's widened eyes.

Anger bubbled inside of Izzy at the idea of this man hurting her only sister. She raised her gun higher, ignoring the pain shooting in her right arm. "Let. Her. Go."

"Can't. Padilla wants you all dead."

Izzy didn't recognize the man's raspy voice.

"Blaire!" Izzy's mother yelled from down the hall.

"Keep her away or your dear mother will die just like your father."

Izzy's breath hitched. "Mom, go back to your room and lock the door!" She focused on the man. "Did you kill my father?"

"I didn't, but I know who did." He sneered. "Let's just say it's someone you'd never guess."

What did that mean? "Tell me more."

Austin edged to the right, keeping his rifle trained on the masked suspect.

The perp angled his gun at Austin. "Stay there." He thrust the gun back into Blaire's temple. "Or she dies."

Névé's low growl rumbled nearby.

The situation had escalated fast. Izzy had to contain the problem or it would end badly.

And she wouldn't let that happen. *Think, Izzy, think. What would you do, Dad?*

A thought entered her mind.

Reason with the man. Talk him down.

"Listen, we're not after you. We want Padilla. Tell us what you can and it will go a long way." Izzy took a baby step forward.

"Right. I don't have a death wish. Not happening. We're here to do a job and get our reward." He pressed the gun harder into Blaire's temple. "Lower your weapons now!"

Blaire whimpered.

Lord, if I do that, my sister is dead. How can I protect her?

Névé let out another deep growl and inched toward Izzy.

Was the K-9 the answer? Izzy shot a glance at Austin and shifted her eyes back to Névé. Then back to him.

She didn't miss his slight dip in his chin.

Izzy lowered her weapon. "Okay, okay. Take me instead. Isn't it really me Padilla wants?"

"You're only part of the deal."

"You said 'we're here.' Who else is on the grounds?" She took another tiny step.

"Padilla has lots of spies. Everywhere." He cocked his head. "Haven't you found that out yet?"

Austin lowered his rifle. "How did you get by my security?"

The masked man gestured toward the opposite side of the room. "First, toss your weapons over there out of reach."

They complied.

Izzy caught Austin's slight flick of his wrist.

Névé changed to a crouching position as if she was about to take a nap, but Izzy knew better. Austin had just given her a special command.

Izzy had to distract the man. "Okay, we did as you said. Answer Austin's question. How did you breach the property and how many are in your party?"

"And did one of my men help you?" Austin added.

"Not one of your men, but someone closely connected." He chuckled. "Padilla has a black hat hacker working for him. He could bypass all your security. You should have learned that the first time it happened."

"I have an armed man patrolling the front gate. Did you hurt him?" Austin's voice raised a notch, the anger evident in his tone.

"Knocked him out. We're not here for your men." He waved the gun toward Izzy. "We're here for the Tremblay family. There's a price on all of your heads. Your father got too close and now you have too. For that, the rest of your family must pay."

Izzy studied her sister. The terror on Blaire's contorted face punched Izzy in the gut. She had to save her. Izzy wouldn't let anything happen to her, not with their broken relationship lurking in the background.

Izzy steeled her jaw and squared her shoulders, mustering courage. She raised her hands. "Let Blaire go. Take me instead."

Blaire shook her head and muffled sounds seeped from beneath the man's hand.

Izzy snuck a peek at Austin.

He gestured toward Névé.

Time to act.

An idea formed. "Blaire, it's going to be okay. Just like that time the boy in high school cornered you. Remember?" Izzy massaged her jaw and stuck out her hip, signaling to her sister what to do. The same actions she did years ago.

Blaire's eyes once again widened, but she blinked twice. Their secret code for yes.

Izzy caught Austin's attention and dipped her head, praying he understood her gesture.

She turned back to her sister and nodded.

Blaire thrust her head upward, catching the man's chin.

He cried out from her sudden movement, releasing his tight hold.

Blaire bit his hand and shoved her hip into him, knocking him away. His weapon fell to the floor.

"Névé, get 'em!" Austin clamped his hand over his opposite arm, signaling a hold tactic.

The dog leaped from her crouched position and barreled toward the masked man. She latched on to his right arm and held.

Once again, the man cried out. "Get this dog off me. I hate dogs!"

Izzy snatched the rifle again and trained it on him. "Okay, Austin."

"Névé, out!" Austin commanded.

The K-9 released her grip.

Izzy moved in front of the man and whipped off his mask, studying his face. "Wait, I remember you. You're the courier who delivers to our station. Tell me who Padilla is."

The twentysomething blond's twisted expression revealed a switch from his earlier sneer to terror. "His clutches reach into prison. I know nothing." He clamped his mouth shut.

Austin yanked the man's arms behind his back, holding him tight.

Izzy set down the rifle. "Blaire, you okay?"

Blaire thrust her arms around Izzy. "Thank you for saving me, sissy."

Austin shoved the assailant toward the door. "Let's go downstairs and wait for the police."

Izzy released Blaire and grabbed the suspect's gun, stuffing it into the back of her waistband.

The man turned from the entrance. "I will tell you that Padilla is coming for you, so beware." He gestured toward Névé and eyed each person slowly. "Not even that mutt can save you from him. All of you are in danger."

Izzy sucked in a breath.

She had to solve this case in order to save everyone she loved.

Austin closed the doors connecting the living room to the hall entrance to give Izzy and Blaire privacy. He left Névé to keep them company and give them an added sense of security. His K-9 had saved the day. Even though she wasn't a guard dog, Austin had trained her on how to subdue and hold. It had taken some time to get Névé to listen and watch his commands, but finally the high-spirited malamute had gotten the tactic correct. This was the first time he had to use it, so Austin was grateful it worked. God was protecting them all.

After Doug and Fisher arrived, they escorted the assailant from the ranch.

The sisters wept and told each other how sorry they were. It seemed the escalated situation had been the catalyst to pave the road to mending their relationship. *Thank You, Lord. Please bring Izzy back to You.*

The constables had failed to catch the other perps, but promised Austin they'd keep an eye on the property for the rest of the evening and overnight.

Sawyer had found the wounded ranch hand and taken him to the hospital to get checked out. Before leaving, he'd ensured the grounds were once again safe.

Austin stepped into the kitchen and stopped short.

Maverick sat nursing a coffee.

Austin's face flushed at the sight of his supposed brother. He quelled the anger burning inside and sat across from him. "Tell me who you really are. No more lying."

"I never lied to you." Maverick studied the coffee steaming in his cup. "I just never said who I really was."

Austin folded his arms and tapped his index finger on his biceps. "Tell me now and leave nothing out. I'm not in the mood."

Maverick sipped his coffee, then set it down. "I'm your brother."

"I don't have a brother." Austin wasn't ready to believe Maverick. Not yet. He required proof.

"Yes, you do. I *am* your brother. Dad died from cancer five years ago. However, a year ago, my—our—mother died in an accident. A tornado whipped through the area and destroyed her home, killing Mom." His voice hitched. "I was working at a nearby ranch when it happened. We were left unscathed."

Austin noted the sorrow in Maverick's voice. He had cared

deeply for the mother and father Austin had never known. "I'm sorry for your loss. My parents died in an accident, so I understand how it feels to lose both."

"I know. I searched for your name, but couldn't find you. Then I guessed your adoptive parents must have changed your last name, so I put in your birth date as Mom told me what it was in her letter to me. I'm good with computers and did an extensive search on everything I knew about you. That's how I eventually found you and the Murray K-9 Ranch."

Austin unfolded his arms. "Wait. If I'm your brother, why haven't you contacted me before now?"

"Because Mom and Dad kept you a secret."

Austin bit the inside of his mouth. Was he that much of a disappointment that they'd remained silent? "Why wouldn't they tell you?"

"No idea. The answer to that question died with them."

"Then how did you find out about me?"

He removed a paper from his shirt pocket and shoved it across the table. "I found your original birth certificate. It was tucked into a letter written to me among my mother's belongings."

Austin unfolded the document and noticed the name.

Austin Jacob Shaw.

His adoptive parents had changed his name to Austin Timothy Murray—after his new father.

He observed Maverick's features. Even though the younger blond didn't match Austin's dark hair, Austin stared into the same blue eyes as his own.

I have a brother!

Doubt once again rose its ugly head as questions filled Austin's mind. "Why didn't you tell me exactly who you were when you arrived at the ranch a month ago? And how did you find me?"

Maverick picked up his mug and finished his coffee before settling his gaze on Austin. "I confess. I was skeptical when I found out I had an older brother. Once I discovered where you were, I applied to be a ranch hand." He huffed. "I guess that part of our bloodline is the same. I really worked on a ranch. Anyway, when I got here, I expected you to be harsh as my employer back at the old ranch."

"And you thought all ranch owners operated the same?"

"Yes."

"My adoptive parents—Tom and Mandy Murray—taught me to respect people. However, it didn't come easy for me." He paused, gathering his thoughts. "I went from foster home to foster home. The last one before I came here was a horrifying experience. My foster dad abused me when I was seven." Austin rubbed the scar above his brow. "That's where this came from. He pushed me down the stairs and I hit my head. Among other beatings."

"I'm so sorry you went through that, and I'm sorry I didn't trust you at first. I quickly realized you're a man of integrity. Your men speak highly of you. I'm proud to call you my big brother."

Austin drew in a sharp breath. "I'm a big brother."

"You are. Can you forgive me for not telling you earlier?"

Words Tom Murray said to Austin many times filtered into his mind.

Son, don't go through life holding back forgiveness. If you do, it will turn into bitterness and God doesn't want that. Forgive as He has forgiven us.

His father had been referring to his birth parents abandoning him and the foster father who had abused him. However, the statement now applied to Maverick. Could he forgive the brother he never knew about?

He searched Maverick's expression for any further deception. But found none.

Austin stood.

Maverick did the same.

Austin embraced his little brother. "Yes." A tear rolled down Austin's cheek. *Thank You, God, for this unexpected gift.*

Maverick withdrew from the hug and took an envelope from a pocket. "One more thing. I also found this among Mom's things." He handed it to him. "I'm heading to bed, but I think you may want to read it. She explained some things to me in my letter and probably did the same in yours."

Austin examined his mother's handwriting.

Austin Jacob Shaw was written on the outside of the envelope.

"Thanks, Maverick. Good night. See you in the morning." He hugged his brother once more. "Thanks for sharing everything with me."

Maverick nodded and exited the room.

Seconds later the front door slammed shut.

Austin plunked down in his chair, disbelief still lingering. He traced his mother's handwriting. Dare he open the envelope? Did he want to put himself through the agony of what was inside on such a stressful day?

Who was he kidding? He had to know.

He ripped open the envelope and removed the letter, unfolding the small page.

Dearest Austin Jacob,

You must have a million questions. I'm sorry for giving you up. I never forgave myself for that and if you're reading this letter, it's because God has taken me home. Let me explain.

I became pregnant at fifteen. I made choices I wasn't proud of and your father—Owen—was older and left for college before I knew I was pregnant. He had broken up with me and cut off all communication. My parents made me put you up for adoption. We were poor, and they said they couldn't feed another mouth. I regretted that decision every day.

Owen returned after college and we rekindled our romance. I told him about you and we tried desperately to find you, but couldn't. We married, and a few years later, Maverick was born. Yes, we should have told him about you, but we didn't want to get his hopes up that he had a brother. We tried searching your date of birth, but it didn't help us narrow down our search at all. I gave up and figured God knew you were happy. I couldn't interrupt that.

Anyway, I just wanted to tell you there wasn't a day that went by where I didn't think of you and wonder about the man you've become, but I'm trusting God worked it all out.

I hope to be reunited with you one day in heaven. I pray every day that you're a believer too.

Son, I love you with all my heart.

Until we meet again,

Mom xo

Tears flowed down Austin's cheeks as he folded the letter and tucked it into the envelope. Emotions flooded him. Years of feeling abandoned dissipated after reading his mother's words. He now knew the truth—

His mother loved him enough to give him up, so he could have a better life.

"Mom, I *will* meet you one day because I know the One you worship," he whispered.

He held his mother's letter to his chest and replayed the conversation he'd just had with his only brother.

Austin straightened as a thought rose.

They had to find Padilla—and fast.

Austin wouldn't lose the last member of his family.

Izzy gripped Blaire's hand as tears clouded Izzy's vision. She blinked them away and breathed in, mustering courage to apologize. She had to take the first step in mending their relationship. Time to swallow her pride and admit any wrongdoing on her part. "I'm sorry I wasn't there for you when Luca broke off your relationship. I failed you. Can you forgive me, sissy?"

Blaire averted her gaze, staring out the window.

The roaring fire crackled, interrupting the sudden silence. Would Blaire forgive her?

Névé nestled herself at Izzy's feet as if anchoring her in place. Izzy loved this dog and didn't know what she'd do when the case was solved. How could she leave Névé when she'd grown attached to the dog—and her handler? The thought brought another wave of tears. *Izzy, Austin isn't interested. Move on.*

Doug had promised to keep Izzy updated on the suspect's interrogation. It frustrated her not to be there, but knew she had to stay away. The board was watching her every move, and she wouldn't put Chief Constable Halt's career in jeopardy again.

After what seemed like an eternity, Blaire cupped Izzy's hand in hers. "Only if you can forgive me. You risked your life to save me tonight, and it made me realize how selfish I've been. None of this was your fault, sissy. Luca deceived me and I put blinders on." A tear slipped down her cheek.

Izzy wiped it away with her free hand. "Love can do that to us. I understand. I didn't mean to get in the way of you coming to that realization yourself."

"You were only trying to help, but I continued to believe his lies." Her eyes hardened. "I won't let any man do that to me again. Ever."

"Blaire, don't close your heart totally."

"Someone needs to listen to her own advice." Blaire tapped her fingers on Izzy's hand. "I can see how you feel about Austin. It's written all over your face when he's in the room."

Izzy puffed out a sigh. "I'm a cop. I should be able to hide my emotions."

"It's hard when it comes to love."

Love? Did she love Austin? She did once. "He doesn't feel the same. He's only ever wanted to be friends."

"Not true. What I see on your face, I see on his when you're around. He worships the ground you walk on." Blaire stroked Izzy's face. "Don't let true love slip away."

Was that what Izzy felt? True love?

Woof!

Névé chose that moment to snuggle closer.

Blaire chuckled. "And clearly this beautiful animal feels the same way."

Was it that simple? Hardly.

"Dad would tell us both to trust God. God knows what's around the corner and has it all planned out for us." Blaire bit her lip. "I'm learning that now. Mom, too, even though it's taken her a bit of time to realize it."

"You're right. He would say that. It's just hard to do. Trusting in Someone you can't see isn't easy." Izzy broke away from her sister's hold and stood, disturbing Névé.

Izzy moved to the window facing the other side of the property and peered into the darkness. Snow sparkled in the ranch's spotlights. Izzy loved the winter's fresh blankets of snow. Its beauty on the mountaintops never failed to make her pause and ponder the greatness of their Creator.

So how could she doubt God when she saw evidence of Him all around her? *He's got you, daughter.*

Words her father told her recently on one of their father-daughter dates.

I'm trying to believe that, Dad.

She turned back to her sister. "Sissy, let's not grow apart again, okay? I've missed you."

Blaire popped upright and embraced Izzy. "Ditto." She broke their hug. "Except I have to tell you my recent news and you won't like it."

"That doesn't sound good."

"You know how I've been growing my skills as a profiler?"

"Yes, and I'm so proud of you. Dad would be too."

"Well, I put in for an opening in the Whitehorse headquarters and I got it. It's a promotion and great for my career." Her lips quivered. "I'm moving, sissy."

No! Just when God gave her back her sister, He snatched her away. Izzy studied the dancing coals in the fireplace, avoiding her sister's eyes as she knew her emotions would be out in the open.

"Say something."

Izzy turned back to Blaire and forced a smile. "I am happy for you. You've been working hard and you deserve it. I'm not sure I can say goodbye. When do you leave?"

"In a month. Mom knows, but I made her promise not to tell you until I could. Uncle Ford knows too."

"Wait, you told Uncle Ford before me?" Izzy failed to subdue the anger in her voice.

"I'm sorry. You and I weren't on the best terms, and Uncle Ford has been there for me."

Izzy dug her nails into her left palm, diverting her frustration. "You're right. I'm sorry." She pulled her sister back into her arms. "I am proud of you. I'm just going to miss you."

"You'll have to visit me. The Yukon is beautiful."

Izzy broke their embrace, and once again sat. "You know how I love the snow, so you won't be able to keep me away. I remember how you took some college trips there. Wait, isn't that where you met the hottie?"

"You mean Dekker Hoyt? Funny. My sergeant suggested I post for the opening and gave me a raving recommendation." Blaire yawned. "I have an important video call with my new sergeant tomorrow morning, so I'm heading to bed. I love you, sissy."

"Love you more."

Blaire opened the double doors and turned from the entrance, smiling. "No, you don't." She blew Izzy a kiss.

"Night." Izzy's shoulders relaxed for the first time all day. She finally had her sister back. For a month.

Moments later Austin appeared in the doorway. "I'm heading to my room and just wanted to say good night. Is Blaire okay?"

Izzy pushed herself upright. "Yes. We had a friendly talk."

"I'm glad. I just had an interesting conversation with Maverick. He is my brother." He waved an envelope in his hand. "I have a letter from my birth mother."

"What? That's outstanding, right?"

"Yes, it's all good. I'll tell you more tomorrow. You need rest. Doesn't the board make their decision in the morning?"

"Don't remind me. Not looking forward to that." She hated that the board held her and her chief constable's careers in their hands.

And she hated that Padilla still walked free. *Lord, if You're listening, show me what I'm missing from those three hours.*

Izzy still had a nagging feeling it was something of vital importance.

SEVENTEEN

After a celebratory breakfast with all his ranch hands and Izzy's family, where Austin introduced Maverick as his brother, Austin carried two fresh coffees into the dining room where Izzy sat. Rebecca and Blaire had gone to their rooms, but earlier talk at the table had been light after such a taxing few days. Even Névé sensed the change in atmosphere. She pranced around the room.

Having Izzy in his home had brought joy back into Austin's life. Joy he hadn't realized he was missing. Even if it was from terrible circumstances, and he knew she'd soon leave after Padilla was caught. Sadness jabbed his heart at the idea of her waltzing back out of his life. *Stay, Iz. I can't bear the idea of life without you.*

However, she didn't feel the same. Her rigid body language whenever he got close proved his theory.

No, Austin had to put a future with Izzy out of his mind. At least, he now had a brother in his life.

Austin set her coffee down. "More caffeine to fuel your day."

"Appreciate it. Keep them coming." Izzy tapped her temple. "There's still something locked in here, and I'm determined to find it." She stood quickly. "Hold on. I just remembered there's one other message we didn't decode. While I wait for the board's decision and for Doug's report on the cookhouse bust, I'm going to take another crack at it." She glanced at her phone. "The temperature is better. You know I think best outdoors, so I'll bundle up and head to your gazebo. It's my favorite spot on your property."

"I'll go with you. I don't want you out there alone. Not with all these break-ins."

Ten minutes later Austin set a thermos in front of Izzy at the picnic table in the middle of the gazebo. She had her father's notes and the Nancy Drew book out.

He leaned his rifle against the gazebo's railing, sat across from her and took a sip from his thermos. "Nothing better than coffee made from freshly roasted beans, especially on a winter day."

She untwisted the lid and inhaled. "Sure smells delightful."

Névé barked.

Austin fished a ball from his winter coat pocket and chucked it across the yard. "She loves running in the snow."

The malamute bounced through the deep snow, chasing the ball. After scooping it up, she barreled toward them.

"I can see that." Izzy's phone rang, and she swiped the screen. "Halt calling with the board's decision, I presume."

Austin shifted to get up. "I'll give you privacy."

She placed her gloved hand on top of his. "No, stay. Please."

He nodded and sat back down.

She hit the speakerphone. "Morning, Chief. What's the verdict?"

"First a quick update on the takedown. We served the warrant to the daughter. She had no idea someone had taken over the old place. Claimed she hated the dilapidated building and never wanted to see it again, so she'd put it out of her mind. Odd. We'll look into her claims and verify her story. Carver reported they breached the premises in the middle of the night and are still investigating the scene. That's all I know at this point."

Izzy tapped her finger on the table. "Okay, and the board meeting?"

"They were lenient on both of us."

Izzy exhaled, her breath vapors rising in the cool air. "Thank God. Did they give a reason for their decision?"

Austin squeezed Izzy's hand.

"Well, the fact that the toxicology report revealed your father was drugged had an enormous influence on their decision. It—"

Izzy blasted upright. "Wait. You finally received the report? When?"

"Moments before the meeting. Sorry, didn't have a minute to call and let you know. You were right all this time, Izzy. The drug caused your dad to have a heart attack, which led to his car accident, according to the coroner." A long sigh sailed through the speakerphone. "I'm just sorry we didn't listen to you from the very beginning."

Izzy plunked down on the bench. "Me too."

"The board did caution us both about not following rules in the future, though, Izzy. They're watching. Mayor Fox still isn't happy."

"Sir, have we found out anything more about her involvement with King & Sons?"

"After the meeting, I confronted her, but she denies everything. I'm not sure, but I think someone may be setting her up to get her out of office."

Austin examined Izzy's scrunched face. He knew that expression well. Her wrinkled forehead revealed her reservations.

She still had doubts about the mayor.

A gust of wind lifted a page from Justin Tremblay's journal.

Izzy slammed her hand on top of the paper to stop it from flying away. "I'm still not convinced, but hopefully, Doug will find out more with the raid. Let me—" She righted the page and leaned closer. "Chief, I gotta go." She ended the call without saying goodbye.

"What is it, Iz?" Austin inched forward. "What do you see?"

She tapped a sequence of numbers. "This is the message I couldn't figure out, but the wind shifted the page in a different direction, giving me a new angle. A new perspective, so to speak."

"I love how God does that."

"I suppose." Izzy bit her lip. "I'm beginning to see God's handiwork, but it's hard."

"It is, but He's there, Iz. You just need to know where to look." Time to change the subject. "What did you find?"

"There are more numbers in this message. Not sure why I didn't notice it before."

"Too much on your mind. What do you think the extra numbers mean?"

"Well, Dad used the book cipher, so I want to follow it again." She opened the book and flipped to the corresponding page, line and word. "The number left is 4."

"What if the 4 represents the letter of the word?"

She snapped her fingers and pointed at him. "You might be on to something there. So the fourth letter is *F.*"

Austin tore off a corner of a page and wrote the letter down.

Névé barked and sped off toward the property line.

"What's gotten into her?" Izzy flipped to another page in *The Hidden Staircase* and searched for the next word.

"Probably an animal. She gets distracted easily sometimes."

"Are all your dogs still okay in the barn? When will the new kennels be ready?"

"Next week. Sawyer and Maverick are with the dogs now. Maverick wants to learn about becoming a K-9 handler and I'm excited to train him." The idea of getting to know his newfound brother sent goose bumps traveling over his entire body. They had talked for an hour earlier this morning, and Maverick revealed his love for dogs.

"That's awesome. I'm so happy for you." She whipped off her plaid flannel scarf. "Wow, it's warmer out than I thought." She stuffed it in her pocket.

"What's the next letter?"

She ran her finger down the page. *"O."*

Austin jotted it beside the *F.*

Izzy turned the pages quickly. "Next is *R.*"

Austin scribbled it onto the page. He stood and observed where Névé had gone, but failed to locate his dog.

Odd.

"Névé, come," he yelled.

Nothing.

Izzy positioned herself beside Austin. "Where did she go? You can go look for her. I'll be okay here."

"I don't want to leave you."

"I'm fine. What can happen?" She gestured toward the rifle. "Besides, I have Beulah here beside me."

"You remembered my rifle's nickname?"

"You forget my perfect—well, almost perfect—memory?"

He chuckled. "Right. Okay, I'm just going to the edge of the property and then back. If I can't find her in five minutes, I'll radio Sawyer." He handed her the pen. "You finish decoding."

"Got it."

Austin prayed for safety and trudged as quickly as he could through the deep snow to the fence line, calling his dog's name.

Névé still didn't answer.

Austin's gut told him to go back to Izzy, but before he could turn around, movement to his right flashed in his peripheral line of sight.

But it was too late.

Someone whacked him from behind.

Stars flickered in his vision as he fell on his back. Snow intermingled with spots moments before he plummeted into the murky darkness.

Izzy eyed the rifle to her right before returning to the last number in her father's code. She riffled through the Nancy Drew book's pages until she found the last letter corresponding with the number. *D.* She wrote it next to the other three and leaned back, studying the word.

FORD

She stood too quickly. Spots twinkled as a memory flashed. The missing piece to the three-hour puzzle.

Her uncle's reflection in the bar's window. He'd been watching that night.

No! Padilla couldn't be her sweet, loving uncle. Sure, they'd been at odds lately, but overall, Uncle Ford had always been kind. Izzy's dad and uncle were inseparable.

She looked at the decoded message once more. FORD. Her father had discovered his brother's betrayal and knew his connection to the police board, so he coded the message to Izzy in his notes.

Izzy plunked back onto the bench and buried her head in her hands, remorse filling her as she thought about how her father must have felt when he learned of his brother's betrayal. *Dad, I wish you would have told me sooner. I could have helped.*

But her father knew he'd be putting his daughter in danger if he brought her in on the case. She lifted her head and snatched her phone. She had to call the chief.

Footsteps crunching on the snow sounded to her right. She stilled and looked up.

Her uncle and an armed man appeared out of nowhere.

"Put the phone down." Her uncle's voice was menacing.

She dropped the phone on top of the paper containing her uncle's name, sprang to her feet and reached for the rifle.

"Don't even think about it." Ford stepped forward. "It's time for you to pay for interfering. Theo, grab the rifle for me."

"Austin!" Izzy had to get his attention. "Help!"

"He can't hear you. He's incapacitated at the moment."

"What did you do to him?" Izzy lunged for her uncle, but he was too quick.

He yanked her injured arm backward.

Pain shot across her shoulders, immobilizing Izzy. *Lord, help me save Austin and Névé! You know how I feel about them. I can't lose them too.*

He sneered. "And his pesky malamute is asleep. I lured her to the fence with food. Don't worry, the drug in the meat was just enough to put her to sleep for a bit. I would never hurt a dog."

Snow mixed with freezing rain pelted Izzy's face. The dark clouds had rolled in while she concentrated on her father's secret message. A message that came too late. "But you killed your own brother?" Fury fueled inside Izzy's body and she fought to contain it.

Izzy, remain calm when your anger wants to guide your actions. Remember your training.

Her father's words bull-rushed her right at the time she needed them most. He had often guided her in her police career.

Theo passed the rifle to her uncle.

"Technically, yes, but Padilla was the one who ordered his execution."

"Wait, you're not Padilla?" She observed the thug standing to the right of her uncle. "Is it you?"

"Pfft! Hardly. Theo does all our dirty work, but now that your team has raided the cookhouse, we'll need to find another spot." He tapped his temple. "I have a new one in mind."

"How did you kill Dad and why, Uncle Ford?"

"Easy. I slipped something into his coffee when he went to the men's room while we were out for our weekly morning breakfast."

Once again, Izzy fought the urge to pounce on her uncle, but she knew he and Theo would overpower her. "So the drug caused him to have a heart attack and crash after he picked up Mom."

"That wasn't supposed to happen. Thankfully, Rebecca wasn't hurt badly." He raised the rifle, waving it at her head. "But you? Your persistent interfering has to stop. I should shoot you right now, but Padilla still wants to talk to you."

"Is Padilla Mayor Fox?" Izzy had to keep him talking. She stole a peek at the barn, but it seemed no one had heard what was happening outside.

"That's not for me to say, and if you're thinking the others will help you, don't. Theo and I piped sleeping gas through Austin's air filtering system in the barn where all his ranch hands were working and in the house. Everyone is out cold. Don't worry, Blaire and Rebecca are fine. I have plans for them."

"What do you mean?"

"I've convinced Padilla they're not a threat. I love your mother and want to marry her. She's another thing my brother stole from me. I saw her first, but he wormed his way into her heart."

Izzy raised her chin, pursing her lips. "She will never marry you."

"Don't be so sure. I'll *save* her from Padilla's men." He air-quoted around the word *save*. "Then she will say yes when I propose. I am a decent human being, though. I will wait a month or two after your funeral."

"You're sick." Izzy's breakfast turned to lead in her stomach, bringing a wave of nausea at the thought of her uncle's actions. "Why? Tell me why you're doing this. Revenge?"

"Partly, but there's something I've kept from the family. Even my dear older brother. I have a love for the slots, but that love has consumed my life. I had to fund my gambling habit somehow, so when Padilla approached me to be the cooker, I jumped at the chance." His cell phone chimed, and he fished it from his pocket. "Time to go."

"I'm not going anywhere with you."

"You will if you want me to leave your boyfriend alive."

"Don't you hurt Austin."

"Then do as I say." He motioned for Theo. "Use your zip ties and secure her."

Think fast, Izzy. Could she leave something behind that would give Austin and Névé a breadcrumb? She remembered the scarf in her pocket. She had to distract them first. "Wait, tell me how long you've been helping this drug ring." She shoved her hands into her pockets.

"Padilla approached me eighteen months ago. Said the current cooker betrayed the organization by skimming money off the top. Had to get rid of him. Padilla found out about my gambling habit."

"How?"

"Padilla has ties everywhere and knows everything. Okay, enough stalling. Let's go."

Izzy made an exaggerated look over her uncle's shoulder, hoping it would distract them.

"What do you see?" Uncle Ford pivoted.

Theo did the same.

Izzy pulled the scarf from her pocket and tossed it on the picnic table's bench.

"Ain't anything there, boss." Theo approached Izzy and fastened her arms behind her, nudging her forward. "Go."

Izzy's pulse thundered in her head as tension corded her neck muscles. "Uncle Ford, where are we going?"

"Not too far. Padilla wants to meet you."

Lord, help!

Theo pushed Izzy toward the property's edge.

Her cell phone rang from its position on the picnic table and faded into the distance as her captors led her through an opening cut into the fence.

The ice pellets turned to heavy snow as the temperature plummeted and a snowstorm threatened the area. Something else to add to the trepidation building inside Izzy.

She set her fears aside and memorized the path in order to retrace her steps.

Izzy prayed Austin could follow their tracks before it was too late.

EIGHTEEN

Pressure weighted Austin's chest. Whines and wet kisses smothered his face as he struggled to clear his foggy brain. Finally registering that Névé was trying to wake him, Austin sat up. He rubbed his eyes and face with the back of his hand. "Girl, you're okay. Where were you?"

She barked, her breath reeking of foul meat.

Had someone lured his dog away with treats?

"Izzy!" Austin brushed off the snow covering his coat, pushed himself to his feet and looked toward the gazebo, which appeared to be empty.

Where was she? He had to find her, but first he had to examine his dog. He squatted and removed his gloves, running his hand along her entire body. "You okay, baby girl?"

Névé barked.

Thank You, Lord.

Austin rubbed the back of his head where someone had knocked him out, and stood. He ignored his anger at himself for allowing the person to get so close undetected and hurried toward the gazebo, removing his two-way radio. "Névé, come."

Austin pressed the button. "Sawyer, Maverick. You there?"

No answer.

He reached the picnic table and noted Izzy's phone. Something was wrong. She wouldn't have left it behind. The piece of paper containing the decoded message flapped in the wind under the phone. Austin read what Izzy had uncovered.

FORD

He gasped. Ford Tremblay was Padilla?

No!

Austin once again hit the radio button. "Sawyer! Maverick! Where are you? Izzy is gone."

The airwaves remained silent.

Austin dug out his cell phone and called Blaire. It went to voice mail.

He hit Doug's number and waited, praying that the team had vacated the cookhouse bunker.

"Carver here."

"Thank God. Doug, Izzy is missing!" Austin failed to contain the panic in his voice.

"Austin, calm down. What happened?"

"Someone lured Névé away, and when I went to look for the dog, I got hit in the head from behind. When I came to, Izzy was gone but her phone is still here in the gazebo. I believe it was her uncle. She decoded the final message and it said FORD."

"What?"

"And I can't get in touch with my ranch hands or Blaire. Can you get here quick?"

An engine came to life, filtering through the phone's speaker. "Yes. Fisher and the team are finishing up at the cookhouse. Everyone was taken to lockup. I'll update Halt. You wait for me before going anywhere. You hear?"

Could Austin promise that? Izzy's life was at stake.

"Austin."

"Fine. I'm heading to the stable to see what's going on. Get EMS here. I believe we'll need them."

"Will do. Be there in ten. Hopefully. The storm is picking up and making the roads slippery. Stay put." Doug clicked off.

At the mention of the weather, a gust of wind picked up an object and swirled it into the air. Austin took a step and snatched it.

Izzy's scarf.

Austin stuffed it into his pocket, then searched around the gazebo. He noted faint tracks heading toward the fence line.

He almost missed them, as the snow had mostly filled them in. Austin counted three sets. One smaller-sized prints and two larger. Austin followed them until he reached the fence. A gaping opening revealed their escape route. Austin banged his hand against his leg. Someone had once again breached his property.

He suppressed his anger and peered through the hole. The tracks headed toward the woods, but stopped. The snow had mostly filled them in. Why hadn't Izzy's abductors taken her to the road and fled by vehicle? He racked his brain, thinking about where these woods led and what buildings were hidden in the forest.

But nothing came to mind.

His radio crackled.

"Austin. You there?" Sawyer's words came through faintly.

Austin pressed the button. "Sawyer! Where are you? What happened?"

"Stable. We were all knocked out by some sort of gas in the air filtration system."

"You okay? What about Maverick and the others?"

"All here and we're sleepy. Just coming to. What's going on?"

"Izzy's been abducted."

Sirens sounded in the distance.

"Help is coming. I'm going to check on Blaire and Rebecca. Meet me there."

"Copy."

Fifteen minutes later, after paramedics and police arrived, Austin ensured his men and Izzy's family were okay. Rebecca and Blaire were presently getting checked by the paramedics. They had refused to acknowledge Ford's involvement. However, Doug and his team would go on that assumption. They hadn't been able to get much out of the men they'd arrested yet, but revealed both the cooker and Padilla weren't present at the raid.

Ford Tremblay fit the bill as a cooker with his chemist's occupation, but the identity of Padilla remained a mystery. Seemed everyone was too scared to snitch on the drug lord.

"Sawyer, can you think of a reason the suspects would take Izzy toward the north forest? I'm trying to rack my foggy brain. There's nothing in those woods, is there?" Austin rubbed the back of his head where he'd been hit. "I've lived here for years, and the only place I can think of is a dilapidated cabin. Surely they wouldn't take her there. It's too obvious."

"I can't think of any other structures, either." Sawyer turned to the men. "Any of you?"

They all shook their heads.

"I also want to know how these men have continually evaded my security." Austin circled the room, studying each face for deception. He stopped in front of Maverick. Surely his brother wouldn't help criminals.

Would he? After all, Austin barely knew him.

Maverick raised his hands. "Wasn't me."

A man to the right of Austin's brother inhaled sharply. "Wait. I remember something. The other day, when Ford was here, he asked me about your ranch and Névé's favorite food. I thought nothing of it because he just seemed interested in your K-9 facility."

"He was obviously plotting then to get the malamute away from you, Austin." Doug addressed the other two officers in the room. "Do another perimeter sweep."

"We already did."

"Do it again!" Doug glanced around the living room. "Where's Fisher?"

One constable shifted his stance. "Said he was called out to do a special task by the chief."

Doug punched his cell phone. "Chief, what do you have Fisher working on?" A pause. The constable's eyes widened. "You didn't?"

Austin stiffened. Not good.

"Let me know if you hear from him. He's MIA." Another pause. "Copy." Doug stuffed his cell phone in his uniform pouch. "Seems Fisher was lying. We'll figure that out later." He pointed to the constables present. "You two split up and search the property."

They nodded and left.

"What did your chief say?" Austin shoved his hands in his coat pocket.

"That he never sent Fisher anywhere. I don't like it, but the man has taken breaks before without telling anyone."

Austin remembered Izzy saying she didn't always get along with Fisher, but that he was a good cop. Odd that he'd show insubordination now in the heat of a major situation and with Izzy missing.

Austin slumped in his chair. *Where are you, Iz?*

Névé positioned her head in Austin's lap as if sensing her handler's sorrow.

Austin fingered her scarf and bolted upright, pulling the flannel cloth out. "We can find her with this and Névé's skills."

"Are you sure you're up to it?"

Izzy was more important than Austin's aching head. "I'm fine. I've got to find her."

"You care for her, don't you?"

"Of course I do. She was my partner."

"It's more than that." Doug tilted his head. "In fact, I've seen the two of you together these past few days, and you're both too stubborn to admit your own feelings. She's not your partner any longer. Take the step. I'm pretty sure you both want to."

Austin sighed. Was the man correct? "I'll sort that out later. First, we need to find her." He turned to Sawyer and Maverick. "You both watch the place and contact me if she returns, okay?"

They nodded.

Austin held the scarf in one hand and snatched his rifle with the other before eyeing his dog. "Névé, come. Time to find Iz."

He prayed the snowstorm hadn't covered her scent.

Austin couldn't lose the woman he loved.

Again.

Izzy huddled in the corner of the chilly log cabin, praying that Austin had found her scarf and was on his way with Doug and Névé. Her uncle and Theo had taken her to a new structure hidden by a wall of Douglas firs behind the old logger's cabin. The scent of fresh lumber told Izzy the building had recently been constructed.

Uncle Ford sat across from her, sipping from a thermos.

She studied his handsome face. How could he have deceived them all, including his own brother? "You deserve an award for your performance all these years. How long have you hated your brother?"

He blew on his nails before rubbing them on his sweater. "I'm good, aren't I?" His eyes darkened. "Growing up, Justin succeeded in everything he did. Sports, school, girls. I was always the second runner-up, but it was after he stole my Becky out from under me that my anger escalated. I took to the casinos and drowned my sorrow at the slots and poker table."

Izzy shifted in the wooden chair and winced from the pressure of her bound hands. She felt around the back of the seat and stubbed her finger on a tiny protruding nail. She cringed, but relief washed through her. *I can use this to help free my hands.* First, she had to stall her uncle. "You're a coward. I can't believe you'd betray and kill your own brother."

"My brother died years ago to me."

How could one child turn out so differently from the other? Even though Izzy and Blaire had their differences, they still worked them out—one by one.

Izzy focused on her surroundings, searching for a way out of the small cabin. She had memorized each step and figured they were approximately two kilometers from Austin's property.

"Why did Padilla build the cabin in this part of the woods?" She slowly rubbed the zip tie against the nail, praying her uncle wouldn't notice.

"The town owns this chunk of the forest, so it was an easy spot to sneak into and hide. Plus no one comes here any longer, so we're going to build an addition and use it for a new cookhouse since you found the one on the Montgomery property." Her uncle chuckled. "Besides, Padilla has an in with the town."

"Are you referring to Mayor Fox?"

"Maybe."

"Who's Padilla?"

Her uncle harrumphed. "You mean, you haven't figured it all out, Miss Perfect Memory?"

"You were present the night Sims was killed. I now remember seeing your reflection in the window."

"I'm shocked it took you that long."

"Boss, Padilla's here." Theo's voice sounded through the radio. Uncle Ford had tasked Theo with guarding the entrance.

Her uncle stood. "Well, now you get to meet our leader and mastermind before you die."

Pounding footfalls stormed the small porch.

The door burst open, bringing a gust of snowy wind.

And someone resembling the abominable snowman.

Padilla shook off the snow and removed a fedora, revealing his balding head.

Izzy's jaw dropped. "You."

No wonder the drug ring could keep one step ahead.

Austin trudged through the deep snow as quick as possible, following Névé into the forest north of his property. The tracks had disappeared under an inch of fresh-fallen snow, so Austin and Doug were trusting the malamute's keen nose and search and rescue skills. After all, Austin had trained Névé hard to make her one of the best SAR dogs in the area. She had found countless lost hikers, especially during the winter months. Malamutes loved this time of year, so Austin had been called upon many times to use Névé's talents.

But right now, his dog was leading them toward the abandoned cabin at the base of a mountain. "This can't be right. She's taking us toward the old logger cabin the town deemed unfit recently and is planning on demolishing in the spring."

Doug ducked under a snow-ridden, low-lying branch. "This area is owned by the town, right?"

"Yes." Austin gripped his rifle tighter. "But I trust Névé. She hasn't failed me yet."

At the mention of her name, Névé stopped, looked back at them and sniffed the air before bounding up the mountain's incline.

Doug's radio squawked a broken message. "King—Son—owned—"

"That's Halt." Doug clicked the button. "Come again."

"Carver! Found—Fisher—Padilla—" The chief's words cut off.

"Ugh!" Doug tried again. "Didn't get that. Repeat."

Static followed by a pop sailed through the radio.

"Normally radios work here." Austin checked his phone. No signal. "Must be because we're deep into the forest, heading up a mountain. Plus the severe weather isn't helping. Do you think he said Fisher was Padilla?"

"I refuse to believe that." Doug adjusted his tuque. "Fisher can be a pain, but he's good at what he does. He wouldn't betray his oath to serve the community."

"Well, money can be a huge temptation to some." Austin searched the woods for his dog. "Where did Névé go?" The radio had distracted him, but he didn't want to call out for the dog for fear of any suspects in the area.

A flash of white and black bounded between trees a few feet ahead of them.

Doug pointed. "There!"

Austin advanced toward Névé and stopped short.

The K-9 had positioned herself beside a tree, growling at something ahead of her.

Austin followed the dog's line of sight.

A figure sat against the decrepit cabin's railing, his gun sitting on his lap.

Austin lifted his right fist in a stop command, then gestured in Névé's direction.

Doug withdrew his gun and nodded, pointing to the left.

Even though Austin hadn't been on the force for ten years, he recognized Doug's intent. He would go left.

Austin raised his rifle and moved right, toward his dog, quickly but in stealth mode—as much as possible in deep snow.

Doug leaned against a tree, raising his gun. "Police! Stand down."

The perp jolted, his gun dropping in the snow.

"Névé, get 'em!" Austin whispered command revealed his intent.

The dog barreled toward the man and latched on to his sleeve.

The suspect cursed. "Get this creature off me!"

Doug sprinted to the man, scooping up his gun. He stuck it in his pocket.

"Névé, out!"

The malamute released her hold.

Doug unhooked his cuffs and secured the thug to the railing. "This will have to do until we can radio for help."

Austin lowered his rifle. "Where's Izzy? Where are they holding her?"

Behind him, Névé growled and took off, running through a wall of Douglas firs.

"She's caught Izzy's scent again. We have to follow." Austin raised his weapon.

"Wait, Austin." Doug yanked on the man's collar. "What's behind those trees?"

"Trouble." He pressed his lips into a flat line, his intent clear. He was done talking.

"I'm following Névé," Austin said. "You coming?"

Doug searched the suspect. He found a cell phone and a radio. Doug shoved them into his own pockets before pushing on the railing. It held. "It's secure." He poked him in the chest. "Don't try anything."

Austin removed his scarf. "Put this over his mouth. We don't want him giving up our presence."

"Open up." Doug shoved it across the gunman's mouth, fastening it at the back of his head. "There. Let's go."

It was now up to Doug, Austin and Névé to save Izzy.

Terror twisted Izzy's stomach at the sight of the drug lord who had also been her father's best friend.

Vincent Jackson—executive member of HRPD's police board.

No wonder he'd been able to stay ahead of the team. Had her father suspected him and that's why he investigated the drug ring in secret? And had Vincent set the mayor up to make it look like she was guilty?

"I fooled even you, Izzy. That crack on your head by Ned sealed the deal and interrupted your perfect memory. I used that to buy time and get to you." He clucked his tongue as he waved his gun back and forth. "However, you proved hard to kill. That stupid handler and his K-9 kept getting in the way. I can't believe I'd been so close to you all this time. I constructed this hideaway to do all my planning, including secret team meetings. Next to Austin's ranch. Who would have thought?"

Izzy gritted her teeth as fury coursed through her, turning her veins to ice. Even though warmth flooded her body from the portable heater, a chill coiled around her spine. A chill permeating from the two evil men in the room. "Seems you weren't as smart as you thought." She continued to saw through her plastic binds with slow, concealed movements. "How could you betray your best friend?"

"Justin? I only got close to him to stay connected at HRPD. Well, that and his recommendation for me to get on the police board." He gestured toward his partner. "That's where I met Ford. I did a deep dive on him and discovered his dirty secret. He loved to gamble, and I knew he was a chemist, so I approached him about becoming my cooker. I guessed the temptation would be too great for him to resist."

Izzy wiggled her fingers, rubbing her wrists together to test the strength of the zip ties. She had made little progress in cutting through. *Keep them talking.* "Why, Vincent? Why bring these bath salts into our community? You're killing teenagers. For money? Is that it?"

A moment of sadness flashed over the man's face, removing his earlier menacing expression. Seconds later it vanished.

"Since you're going to die, I'll tell you *my* dirty little secret. I had an affair with Georgia years ago."

Izzy drew in a sharp breath. That was the connection to the mayor.

"This all happened before she took office. She broke it off with me when she found out she was pregnant, stating she wanted to work things out with her husband." Once again, his eyes softened. "I was in love with her and she broke my heart."

"But what has all that got to do with your drug ring?"

"When Georgia delivered the baby, she knew right away our child had special needs. She was planning on running for mayor, so she contacted me to let me know she wanted to put our baby up for adoption." The man's face reddened as the vein in his neck popped.

Izzy read Vincent's expression. "And that made you angry."

"Yes! She was going to abandon our baby all for her stupid candidacy. I told her right away I would take our baby girl. I put her in a special needs home and kept our secret." He hissed out a breath. "I soon found out I needed more money than my job would give, so I hatched a plan to make more. Took me a while to put it into motion. You know the rest."

His child's needs made Izzy feel bad, but that didn't give him the right to kill. "I'm sorry about your child, but you've taken lives. Do you think your daughter would really want you to do that?"

"You know what they say—the end justifies the means." His eyes once again hardened. "And Georgia will pay for her part in this."

"You set her up to take the fall? Let me guess, you put the ownership of King & Sons in her name?"

"Smart girl. But your father got too close, and we had to eliminate him." He gestured toward Izzy's uncle. "Ford didn't flinch when I ordered him to do it."

Her uncle smirked.

"You're lucky my hands are tied right now." Izzy turned back to Vincent. "How did you infiltrate HRPD's systems and Austin's?"

"I have a black hat hacker on speed dial. He's the best in the region." Vincent checked his watch before addressing her uncle. "They should be here soon."

Her uncle moved to the front window. "Good guess. I see a couple of shadows out there and a dog."

Izzy stilled. "What are you talking about?"

Her uncle turned, a smug smile appearing on his face. "You didn't think we only wanted you, did you?"

Lord, no!

NINETEEN

Austin stepped through the trees, following Névé with Doug at his side. Austin's elevated heartbeat ratcheted up with the sight before them.

A newly constructed cabin lay hidden among more trees.

Even though it was midmorning, the storm had darkened the forest, preventing them from seeing clearly, but a glow coming from the cabin revealed it was occupied.

A shadow skulked by the window holding a gun.

This had to be Padilla's hideout.

"What's the plan?" Austin kept his voice low.

Doug hit his radio button and requested backup, giving them their location. However, only a crackle answered. He tried again, but no one acknowledged his call for help. "Ugh!"

Austin tried his two-way again, but it was useless. They were too deep into the woods. Plus the mountains were impeding the signal. "We have to help Izzy."

Doug gestured toward the cabin. "You check around back for another entrance and whistle when you find one. I'll whistle back in acknowledgment." He pointed to the door. "I'll position myself there." He gestured toward the K-9. "Can she bark on command?"

"Of course."

"Get her to bark when you're ready. I'll breach first, then you enter. I realize you're trained, but it's been a few years." He paused. "If there's no other entrance, return here and we'll go in together. We can't wait for backup since my radio isn't cooperating. Let me lead, okay?"

Austin nodded. "Névé, come." He crouch-walked to a tree on the right with his dog at his heels. *Lord, protect us all!*

Austin and Névé moved to the rear, and he spotted another door. He whistled, praying no one inside heard.

Doug returned the whistle, sending his signal.

Austin reached the entrance and positioned himself to the right, raising his rifle. Before giving the command, Austin prayed. *Lord, I'm sorry I sometimes doubt Your plans. Please forgive me. You know I love Izzy. Even if You don't bring her back into my life, please save her. Don't let her die. Give me strength not to hesitate this time. I choose to trust You fully. No matter what.*

Austin inhaled and turned to his dog. "Névé, speak!"

The K-9 barked.

He waited until he heard Doug breach the front and yell, "Police! Stand down."

Austin kicked in the door, pointing his weapon.

"Well, it's about time you arrived." A voice snickered. "We've been waiting."

What?

Austin scanned the tiny one-room cabin. A couch sat at one end with a rocker next to it. A table and chairs formed the small kitchen area.

Ford stood over Izzy with a gun pointed at her temple.

Vincent Jackson tilted his head, raising his weapon higher. "Welcome to the party."

"You're Padilla?" Austin advanced farther into the cabin.

"I am and my spy here was right." His eyes shifted to Ford. "He said you'd come because you're in love with his niece."

Austin's gaze locked with Izzy's.

Her lips quivered, and she looked up at Vincent. "Leave them out of this! It's me you want."

"Give it up, man. Our team is on the way." Doug took a step forward.

Vincent waved his gun toward the sofa. "Drop your weapons, gentlemen, and have a seat, or the beautiful Isabelle Tremblay will die."

Her uncle thrust his Glock into Izzy's temple.

"You'd hurt your niece? You're sick." The scene with Clara and Izzy flashed through Austin's mind. He would not hesitate. *You've got this.*

Beside him, his K-9 continued her low menacing growl. Clearly, she sensed the danger of the situation.

Doug remained planted in place. "How about you two lower *your* weapons first? Let's talk this through. Tell us what you want."

The constable was stalling for time, but for what? Their cry for help went unanswered. No one was coming.

Austin returned his attention to Izzy.

She turned her head slightly and lowered her eyes, looking behind her.

It was then he noticed her slight movements. She was trying to free her hands.

And he had to buy her time.

"How did you get onto my ranch so easily?" Austin kept his grip on his rifle tight, ready to fire at a moment's notice. "Did you buy off one of my men?"

"I can answer that." Ford shifted his stance. "I hinted at it with one of your men, but he proved loyal to you. But I got out of him what treat your dog likes and good information regarding your ranch."

"Did you set fire to my kennel?"

"Of course, but only to get you out of the ranch house. I trusted you'd stop the fire. I wouldn't purposely kill a dog. I just had to buy time to steal my brother's journal notes and the drive."

"Unbelievable." Austin subdued the anger boiling inside and stole another glimpse of Izzy.

She gave him a slight nod, showing she was ready.

But how could they overpower two armed men? Plus warn Doug?

A thought rose. He lifted his rifle higher. "Well, seems we have a standoff here. Reminds me of the case we worked on eleven years ago, two towns over." His eyes caught Izzy's.

She dipped her chin in acknowledgment.

He knew her perfect memory wouldn't let her forget her actions that day.

Austin caught Doug's attention and tapped his index finger on his rifle toward Izzy, praying the man would catch his drift.

Doug turned to Izzy, giving his head a slight nod.

Time to strike.

Austin said a quick prayer and braced himself with what he knew she was about to do. "Now!"

Izzy leaped from her chair and plowed into her uncle, taking him off guard.

Ford's gun discharged before it clattered to the floor.

Doug dropped.

"No!" Izzy pushed her uncle hard to the right.

Vincent—aka Padilla—aimed his gun at Izzy. "Time to die, little girl."

"Névé, get 'em!" Austin gestured toward Ford.

The dog catapulted through the air, taking Ford off guard.

Austin aimed his rifle at Vincent. "Stand down or I'll shoot."

Padilla turned his gun on Austin.

This time, Austin didn't hesitate. He fired at the same time as Padilla, hitting him in his forehead.

The man collapsed, his lifeless eyes staring at the ceiling.

Pain burned Austin's leg, registering Padilla's aim had also met its target.

Austin dropped his rifle before sinking to the floor.

"No!" Izzy fell by Austin's side. "Don't leave me." Tears clouded her vision.

Austin clutched his leg. "I'm okay. Get weapons. Check Doug." His forced, broken words revealed his pain.

Izzy scrambled to Doug and turned her unconscious partner over. Blood seeped from his right shoulder. She applied pressure. "He's bleeding badly. When is help arriving?"

"They're not. We bluffed." Austin winced. "No reception."

"What?"

Her uncle snickered. "They'll both bleed out before anyone finds us."

Névé growled and seized the man's sleeve, holding him tight. "Get this dog off me!"

"Let him suffer, Austin." Right now, Izzy didn't care about her uncle. She pressed harder on Doug's wound. "What are we going to do?"

"I can go for help." Austin crawled to the couch and tried to push himself upward, but fell back down, yelling in pain.

Izzy spotted the trail of blood he left on his way to the couch. "You're not going anywhere. I'll go."

"But do you even know where you are?"

"I memorized the path we took to get here." She noted Doug's paling complexion. "He's losing too much blood. If I can get to the edge of the clearing, I can call for help."

A contorted expression flashed on Austin's face.

Izzy remembered he had shared his fear of abandonment because his biological parents had given him up as a baby. "I'm coming back, Austin. I won't abandon you or Doug."

His shoulders slumped. "I know." He pointed to Névé. "Take her with you. She'll listen to your commands."

"But what about my dear old uncle?"

"Tie his hands and feet to a chair. Hand me Ford's Glock and I'll keep guard." He maneuvered his way to Izzy's side. "I'll apply pressure on his wound."

Izzy released her hold.

Austin pressed on the injury with his left hand.

She rummaged through Doug's pockets. "Where are his cuffs?"

"Securing one of Padilla's men by the old logger's cabin."

Izzy snatched her uncle's gun from the floor, handing it to Austin. She hurried to the tiny kitchen and searched the drawers. Finding rope, she examined the other wooden chair for protruding nails. "Good, this one doesn't have a nail. I guess you should have thought to look before pushing me into a chair that had a means of escape." She hauled it over to where Névé had her uncle subdued. "Névé, out!"

The dog released him.

She pointed to the chair. "Sit."

Her uncle glared at her, defying her command.

Izzy kicked behind his knees, and his legs buckled. She shoved him into the seat, yanking both arms behind his back with all the force she could muster.

She ignored his audible wince and secured his hands with the rope, looping it through the chair. She did the same to his feet before positioning herself in front of him. "You will pay for killing my father. I will make sure the judge comes down hard on you. My mother will never marry you now."

He spat in her face.

Izzy resisted the urge to punch the man, but wiped her face with the back of her hand. She wouldn't do anything to jeopardize putting her uncle behind bars. "I won't stoop to your level."

She approached Austin and squatted to face him. "You sure you'll be okay?"

"God's got me and you. Believe, Iz." His lips turned upward into the smile she'd always found hard to resist.

"Austin, I—"

"Go, Iz. Doug needs you. We can talk later."

Izzy traced his lips with her fingers. "I will be back for you." She pocketed Doug's radio before snatching up his gun and moving to the door. "Névé, come."

The dog ignored her command and trotted to Austin's side, licking his face.

"I love you too, baby girl. I'll be fine." He pointed to Izzy. "Névé, heel."

The malamute whined but raced toward Izzy, obeying her handler.

Izzy put on her gloves and opened the door.

A gust of wind blew icy snow into her face, but she pressed

forward with Névé at her side. Izzy ran as fast as she could through the deep snow, retracing her steps. *Memory, don't fail me now.*

God's got you. Believe, Iz.

Austin's words returned to her like a beacon from a lighthouse on a stormy night.

Was he right? Was it time to believe?

God, I've questioned Your path for my life. I'm stubborn and thought I could do it all on my own. Thought I knew better than You. I've taken the wrong roads, haven't I? I'm sorry.

She wiped a tear away. *I surrender my life back to You. Take it and do what You will with me, but please help me to get out of the forest quickly. Doug and Austin need medical attention.*

After ten minutes of slogging through the snow, they came to a fork in the woods. She searched her memory. *Right, Izzy.* She stepped forward, but Névé barked and tugged on the bottom of her coat.

"What is it, girl? This is the way I came."

The dog barked again and bounded to the left.

What was Névé telling her? Should she trust in her own memories or the SAR dog? *Show me, Lord. I'm bad at trusting.*

Névé stopped and glanced over her shoulder, barking ferociously as if saying, "Follow."

"Okay, girl. You lead the way."

Ten minutes later Izzy and Névé reached the edge of the woods. "You knew a shortcut, didn't you?"

Névé barked and bounded into the clearing.

Thank You, God, for this amazing dog.

Izzy followed the malamute and once they cleared the forest, she pulled out her partner's radio. "Dispatch, this is Constable Isabelle Tremblay." She stated her badge number and waited, praying for good reception.

"Tremblay, go ahead," Dispatch said.

"Officer down and civilian wounded. Need emergency medical assistance and evac." She gave Dispatch her location.

"Izzy, you're okay?" Chief Constable Halt's voice blared through the speaker.

"Yes, sir. They shot Doug and Austin. Padilla is down and my uncle, Padilla's cooker, is secured."

"Fisher is at the ranch. I'll send him to your location and get paramedics to you stat. Hold tight."

"Get here fast! Doug has lost a lot of blood."

"On our way."

Névé whimpered.

Izzy tucked the radio into her pocket and squatted in front of the dog. "Austin will be okay, girl. I promise." She hugged the malamute tightly and prayed for the Lord to save the man she loved.

Thirty minutes later Izzy reached the cabin with Constables Fisher and Reynolds, and two paramedics. She'd taken them there via Névé's shortcut.

Izzy dropped at Austin's side, her shoulder slumping in relief that he was still conscious.

"You're back faster than I thought you'd be." Austin smiled.

However, his pale complexion told Izzy his condition had worsened. She rubbed his arm. "Névé got me out through a shortcut. She's one smart dog."

Névé responded by licking her handler's face.

While the paramedics attended to Doug, Fisher had explained his earlier absence to Izzy and Austin. He had gotten a tip from an informant and had to respond in secret. The information had led him to the mayor's office, where she confessed that she had lied. Her anonymous tip about Izzy's actions had come from Vincent.

"That doesn't surprise me knowing what I know now." Izzy gestured toward her uncle. "Can you get him out of my sight?"

"With pleasure." Fisher left their side.

Izzy sat beside Austin. "I have to talk to you before the paramedics check your wound." She shifted herself closer to him. "I wanted you to know I don't blame you for Clara's death. I did—

at first—but my dad helped me see it was only the assailant's fault. Not yours." She rubbed the stubble on his chin. "It's time for you to forgive yourself."

"Iz, I do now. God has shown me I need to put the past where it belongs. In the past. I only froze because the situation took me back to a beating my foster father gave me. It was a night I almost died." He paused, as if gathering his thoughts. "I was also going to tell you something the night Clara died, but never got the chance. Then we drifted apart, and it's taken God ten years to bring you back into my life." Tears welled before he continued. "I don't understand why God chooses some circumstances to take longer than others, but what I do know is, He knows best and I trust His timing. I trust in His journey for me. For us." Austin took her hands in his. "I want you in my life, but as more than friends."

Névé barked as if agreeing with Austin's statement.

Izzy chuckled. "That's funny, because I was going to tell you the same thing that night. I was done fighting my feelings for you and planned to ask for a transfer."

"Well, I guess God had something else in mind."

Something better. "I'm sorry for pulling back the past few days. I dated a man who became obsessed with me and I vowed not to get involved with anyone else, but then you stole my heart. Again."

"Sorry. Not sorry." He chuckled as his gaze dropped to her mouth. "Will you go out on a date with me, Iz?"

"Yes." Izzy didn't hesitate, but tilted her face upward and leaned forward, meeting his lips with hers in a tender kiss.

Beside them, Névé barked.

Izzy chuckled, but kept her lips firmly on his. She had waited ten years for this kiss, and she wanted to relish the moment.

After all, God had not only given her the man of her dreams and a dog she loved, but planted her firmly on His path for her life.

And she planned to trust Him with everything.

EPILOGUE

Sixteen months later

Austin climbed the steps of the stage on the Murray K-9 Ranch's backyard. He stepped into the middle of an archway adorned with pink and red roses. Maverick positioned himself on one side of Austin. Sawyer on the other. His two best men. Austin wouldn't have it any other way on his wedding day.

Névé bounded up the stairs and planted herself in front of Austin, turning to face the crowd sitting in chairs lining the back lawn.

"Névé, speak," Maverick commanded.

She barked, signaling her approval to let the ceremony begin.

The small gathering consisting of family and close friends laughed.

Austin smiled. Everything was perfect for their wedding, even the clear blue June day sky.

He thought back over the past sixteen months and marveled at God's handiwork. Not only had Doug survived his injuries, but the constables were able to round up all of Padilla's men after Ford confessed everything. He was convicted of killing his brother after police found the drug used in his condo and Vincent's text telling him to murder Chief Constable Justin Tremblay. They had also discovered ingredients in his garage, linking him to the drug cookhouse. His fate was sealed.

Izzy grieved the loss of her uncle, but became closer to her mother and Blaire. The family's bond was now unbreakable, even after saying goodbye to Blaire as she relocated to the Yukon.

Austin and Sawyer had trained Maverick hard with the dogs,

teaching him everything they knew. He excelled quickly and agreed to stay on the ranch. After Austin had proposed to Izzy, the two men, along with the ranch hands, built a cabin at the other end of the extensive property for Sawyer and Maverick to share. Austin had teased them, stating it was a temporary living arrangement until they found the women God had planned for their lives.

Both had said it wouldn't happen. They were happy being single.

But Austin guessed God probably had other journeys in store for them.

The guitarist strummed on the fretboard, declaring the start of the ceremony, before playing a soft tune.

Blaire Tremblay emerged from around the two large trees in the backyard, holding her flowers that matched the archway Austin stood under. She had made the trip back to British Columbia from the Yukon to witness her sister's—and best friend—wedding. She slowly made her way to the front.

The pianist joined in with the guitarist, announcing the bride's entrance.

The crowd rose to its feet.

Izzy appeared with her mother by her side, smiling from ear to ear.

Austin couldn't contain his soft gasp. Her beauty mesmerized him. Dressed in a flowing, strapless white gown, she took his breath away. Her hair was swept into a crown of curls with a tiny tiara tucked inside, sparkling in the sunlight.

Izzy stopped at the row of constables dressed in their uniforms. She kissed Doug's and the chief's cheeks before continuing to the front. She stopped at the base of the stairs.

"Who gives this woman to this man?" The pastor's voice boomed through the microphone.

"Her father and I." Rebecca Tremblay kissed her daughter's cheek and placed Chief Constable Justin Tremblay's badge into the center of Izzy's bouquet.

The perfect way to honor her fallen father.

Austin moved to the front and walked down the steps, holding out his hand.

Izzy kissed her mother's cheek before taking Austin's hand and walking up the stairs.

They stood under the arch, facing each other, with Névé sitting in front of them.

"You're beautiful," Austin whispered.

She chuckled. "Well, you clean up nicely, my handsome rancher. I love you with all my heart."

"Love you too." Austin smiled, taking in his surroundings and the moment.

God had answered all his prayers. He gave Austin a woman he adored, and a family he had longed for all his life.

Austin only needed to wait for God's perfect timing because He really did know best.

* * * * *

If you liked this story from Darlene L. Turner,
check out her previous Love Inspired Suspense books:

Border Breach
Abducted in Alaska
Lethal Cover-Up
Safe House Exposed
Fatal Forensic Investigation
Explosive Christmas Showdown
Alaskan Avalanche Escape
Mountain Abduction Rescue
Buried Grave Secrets
Yukon Wilderness Evidence

Available now from Love Inspired Suspense!
Find more great reads at LoveInspired.com.

Dear Reader,

I really appreciate you reading Izzy, Austin and Névé's story! These are new characters, and I hope you enjoyed getting to know them and the others in this book like I did. You never know when some of them will show up in another book. I also loved creating the fictional town of Harturn River, British Columbia. The name comes from a combination of my maiden name Harrison and my married name Turner—Harturn River.

Izzy and Austin both wrestled with trusting that God was in control of their life's journey. They found it hard to see His path. This is something we all can relate to, can't we? I'm so thankful He's the one in control.

I'd love to hear from you. You can contact me through my website www.darlenelturner.com and also sign up for my newsletter to receive exclusive subscriber giveaways. Thanks again for reading my story.

God bless,
Darlene L. Turner

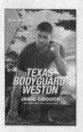